THE LUST LIST: DEVON STONE

THIRD DEGREE

MIRA BAILEE

NoMi Press

Euphoria Publishing
NoMi Press
www.euphoriapublishing.com

Publisher's Note: This is a work of fiction. Names, characters, places, and incidents are a product of the author's imagination, and any resemblance to actual people, living or dead, or to businesses, companies, events, institutions, or locales is completely coincidental.

ISBN-13: **978-0692383162**
ISBN-10: **0692383166**

Printed in the United States of America

For everyone who hasn't yet experienced

their fifteen minutes of fame.

CHAPTER ONE

The perfect remedy for a Devon Stone hangover involves gourmet cupcakes with edible glitter and a best friend—not that it was an easy feat getting to this moment.

Last week, I walked away from Devon, and I still stand by the idea that it was for the best. After I called Maddie from the bus station asking her to pick me up, she spent the entire trip back to our little apartment giving me the third degree.

In one quick breath, as though each question was fighting the others to escape Maddie's lips first, the words plummeted out.

"Where were you? What were you doing? And how did you misplace a Stone twin in the process?" Never mind that she spent more time watching me than looking at the road.

I tried my best to summarize it without making Devon look horrible. I explained how we went to Bandon, Oregon in search for his mother who he'd always been told was dead. Unfortunately, she really was. And more unfortunately, we discovered the existence of Lex, Devon's long-lost half-sister who wants nothing to do with him.

"She slammed the door in our faces. Twice," I told Maddie while watching the road on her behalf. It was like her car was equipped with some sort of force field. The woman drove like a stunt driver, seamlessly switching lanes and ignoring her speed, yet everyone made room for her—a very abnormal occurrence in LA traffic.

"Ouch," Maddie said. "Did that cause you two to fight after or something?"

Or something. I remembered the previous night and all the pleasure Devon had brought me. We'd collided as though we'd been starving from lust. Our legs intertwined, and our bodies connected as though we'd been created only for each other. How could such a passionate night transition to a dark, ugly morning?

"Devon is a drug addict," I said bluntly, letting my gaze drift out the window. Saying it felt foreign. He's so powerful. He could do anything. Why does he think he has to do drugs?

Maddie made a quick turn onto our road and shrugged. "I'm sorry. Unfortunately, it was already pretty obvious by what the tabloids all said. I mean, *ScandalLust*—"

"I don't care what *ScandalLust* reported. I care that *he* told me he wasn't doing that stuff anymore. He promised." I took a deep breath. "He lied."

We pulled into our complex in silence. I retrieved the duffle bag from the trunk as a thought occurred to me. Holding Maddie's bright pink bag she'd loaned me, I looked from it to her and asked, "If you knew about him, then why were you so eager to have me go away with him?" She's always first to stand up for me. She could have prevented all this trouble by speaking up.

She let us into the apartment, stopping in the living room. "Because a bad decision isn't the end of the world. He's been through a lot. *You've* been through a lot. I think you two could help each other. But you have to confront the bad before you can both heal. You'd be his new drug. He'd be your therapy."

Philosophical Maddie. Always the romantic.

Now, one Monday later, we're camped out on the sofa, eating breakfast cupcakes—yes, I've determined that's a "thing"—and watching the highlights of the HIT Awards Maddie recorded over the weekend. The sometimes funny, sometimes cringe-worthy comedian,

Jamal Mason had hosted the music awards show, and the recap we're watching is listing his best and worst jokes of the night.

"We should've come up with some sort of drinking game before watching this," Maddie says. She's wearing pink flannel pajamas, thick-framed glasses instead of her contacts, and her blond hair is in a knot on her head.

As if it's not already obvious, I remind her, "It's only 10:00 a.m."

"Yeah? And we're eating cupcakes." She pokes at the icing and licks it off her finger. "Delicious, delicious cupcakes."

I glance toward the box on the coffee table. White with a gold cupcake logo. I'd brought home a half dozen, and two remained.

"You said you got these for free?" Maddie asks.

I'd gone in with the intention of getting two, one for each of us. I came out with the box and didn't have to spend a penny. Usually, six of these gourmet bad boys would've been as much as a tank of gas. "Yeah, it was awesome. The girl behind the counter got all excited when she saw me. Then she called her boss to the front. It was the owner who insisted."

"That's so weird."

"Nah. Devon said this kind of stuff would be normal from now on." In the car ride up to Oregon, he'd mentioned it was just part of the lifestyle. Apparently, people know who I am now.

Maddie sighs. "I want to be a celebrity."

"I am *not* a celebrity." I point to the TV. "They are."

The camera switches from the crowd of big name Hollywood elite back to the main stage. A single spotlight lands on a guy with a guitar—Ethan Beckham.

"Olivia! You have to watch this. He's so damn hot."

His dark hair and tattoos make him look rough, but his glasses—which look just like Maddie's—bring him back to "hot, next door neighbor" status. He has a band of people behind him, lit up in red. The effect makes it all seem so sexy, so mysterious. But the stories about this guy aren't too kind. He's known for being egotistical and rude. And the fact that I know this is a little alarming. It means I've been holed up in this apartment too much the past few days. I've been binging on bad TV and junk food.

I look around the place. A few dirty dishes on the counter, but it's otherwise clean. There's still hope for me yet. Note to self: Get the hell out of the apartment...soon.

Maddie stares dreamy-eyed at the TV, watching Ethan Beckham strum his guitar and make eye contact with the camera.

"I heard he's an asshole," I say.

She doesn't miss a beat. "Aren't they all?" It doesn't stop her from practically drooling on her German chocolate truffle cupcake.

Her comment sends one image into my head—Devon. His sexy smirk, his messy hair, his strong hands gripping my hips. I shake my head to evict the thought. "I can't think of any instances that have proven otherwise. Take it from me, you need to find a nice, down-to-earth guy who'll treat you well and not hide all his baggage." I stuff my last bite into my mouth as though it's the final point to my argument.

She laughs. "Yeah...because *that* doesn't sound boring. Take Corey, for instance—"

"You're still seeing him?" I think back to when he was wandering around the apartment in his underwear. He's a good-looking guy, though a little dense. I hadn't seen him since, so I'd assumed he'd been a one-night tryst.

"I am. Is that a problem?"

"Not at all. I just haven't heard much about him. He hasn't been here since..." Since the day Devon showed up asking me to go on a trip with him. Dammit. All roads lead to Devon. This is precisely why I've been hiding out here. I can't even hang out with my best friend without everything reminding me of him.

"We've gone on a few dates, and I stayed at his place the other night. You should see his condo. It's double the size of this place— huge!"

That's how these people roll. They live large with, seemingly, no care in the world.

"Look. It's your boyfriend's brother."

"Let's not throw the B-word around." I look up at the screen to see Kaidan in the audience.

"What? *Brother?*" Maddie gives me a mischievous grin, and I chuck a pillow at her. It hits the hand holding her cupcake, smashing it into her chin. Her icing beard sets me off into a giggle fit as Maddie rushes over and gives me an overly enthusiastic hug, leaving cupcake remnants in my hair. Now that we both look like hot messes, she settles in next to me as they continue to focus on Kaidan Stone.

"Aren't highlight shows supposed to get to the point and show the actual, you know, highlights?" I ask, more of a criticism than a query.

"I don't know," Maddie says. "Look at him in that tux. He looks like a highlight to me."

I laugh as we watch Devon's twin stand up. The shaky camera footage zooms out to show a girl from that show, Werewolf Chronicles, looking pissed off. I don't know what she does in the music industry—if anything—but she looks like she missed out on an award and is ready to retaliate. The camera pans over to someone else, a blond woman.

"Hayley Wade," Maddie states.

"Kaidan's girlfriend," I confirm.

Hayley's wearing a spectacular gown that looks like it came from another era. But before I have time to truly admire it, the Werewolf chick stomps over and dumps a glass of wine on her head.

"Whoa!" Maddie and I shriek in unison. We're glued to the TV now as Calvin Stone steps in. His fury permeates through the screen and right into our living room. What the hell is going on?

Hayley looks mortified. The angry blond looks like she's about to pounce. And Kaidan Stone is quickly removing his tux jacket to cover Hayley. Oh hey, there you go. Proof that they all don't act like assholes all the time. What's with these guys? They bring about so much trouble and uncertainty, yet in the next instant, their entire focus is on you and defending your honor. Kaidan and Hayley leave the building, flanked by security detail. The camera tries to get closer to Calvin, but the head of Stone Records gives an icy glare, and the camera cuts off.

Back to the recap hosts. One is covering her face as though she just lived through that embarrassing experience while the other laughs and says, "The attack they didn't want you to see. That footage was never going to make the final cut, so you saw it from us first." She turns to her co-host and they try to dissect the details, but with only brief footage to work from, their theories are forced. They come to the assumption that Kaidan's been dating both women, and the HIT Awards is where the truth came out.

"And you thought your relationship had too much drama," Maddie says.

I nod in agreement. I guess that's one point for Devon. At least he's never humiliated me in front of the entire world.

"You should reach out to her." Maddie peels her gaze from the drama on TV to look at me. "You could start a Stone brother support group."

"No way. We're on entirely different levels. She actually belongs in the Stone world with her rock star dad and money and all. Me? I..."

"Belong with Devon." Maddie looks at me seriously. She managed to get most the icing off her face, but a tiny spot remains. I focus on that in order to avoid reality right now. "You should call him."

Call him...And then what?

"I'm not calling him. It took everything for me to stick up for myself. I can't be with a liar. And I won't be with someone who's so irresponsible when it comes to coping with his problems. Think of my problems?" My anxiety, my depression, my inability to find closure after my brother's death. "You think his habits would have a positive effect on me?"

Maddie sits in silence. I wish it were easier. I wish I could call him, forgive him, and move on. But it's Devon's turn. He's the one who has to decide what our relationship is worth.

"Then hopefully you'll hear from him soon," she says.

My phone rings.

We both jump and stare at each other.

"If you have creepy mind powers I don't know about, you should warn me now."

Maddie laughs as I grab my phone. The screen says "unknown", so I answer.

"Olivia Margot?" a woman's voice asks.

"This is she," I say. It must be another random job offer. Being connected to the Stones isn't all that bad.

"My name's Natalia Vorhees. I don't know if you remember me. We met on the bus, very briefly. I was sitting a row behind you and asked about you and Devon."

I did remember. She'd shown me her computer screen with the *ScandalLust* headline of the day. She'd told me how lucky I was to be Devon's girlfriend. I still wasn't feeling that lucky though.

"How'd you get my number?"

"I know, I know," she says. "This is really bizarre. I work with people who make it easy to get ahold of who I need to contact. I promise, this is genuine. I need to meet with you."

Seriously? This can't sound crazier. Like hell am I going to meet up with some random fan girl who tracked me down after ten seconds of talking to me.

"Your silence tells me you're feeling skeptical," she says.

Yeah, no crap.

"I'm not sure it's a good idea. I—uh—I don't have a lot of free time." I look around my apartment again and back at the TV where Bia is front and center, looking gorgeous on the red carpet. "I'm pretty busy."

"I can work around your schedule. Whatever you'd like. I just need five minutes of your time to talk to you about something."

I begin to object again. "Thanks, but—"

"It has to do with Jared."

I swear my heart leaps from my chest, right into my throat. My words catch. Who is this woman? How does she know about my brother? Why does she want to talk to me about him?

"Fine," I say. "We can meet tomorrow. Where?"

Natalia gives me the name of a cafe in downtown LA. I tell her I'm bringing a friend, and I'll see her at noon. She says she'll buy me lunch, and I hang up, a lump still caught in my throat.

"You look like you've seen a ghost. What's wrong?" Maddie looks concerned, but I can't comprehend what just happened. "What is it, Olivia?"

"I'm not sure." I take a deep, calming breath. "But we have lunch plans for tomorrow."

CHAPTER TWO

The next morning, my heart is racing. My alarm goes off to tell me it's time to leave. Maddie is being extra supportive by not asking questions, but I sense the excitement emanating from her. She loves mystery and adventure. This is a field trip for her. For me? I hate the unexpected, and Natalia was all too vague on the phone.

I let Maddie drive, and halfway there, Natalia calls again, requesting a venue change.

"Bella's is even closer to you and has great Italian food. I hope you don't mind. I'll order us a bottle of wine to be our icebreaker."

Wine sounded good at the moment—something to settle my nerves. I tell Maddie the new location, and fifteen minutes later, we park. I take a quick look in the visor mirror and fix an eyeliner smudge. Aside from running quick errands, this is my first time out in public since walking away from Devon. I think I was scared I'd be recognized and then questioned about our relationship. I didn't even have those answers for myself.

"You look good. Let's go." Maddie opens her door and gets out. She's wearing a long-sleeve shirt with a short skirt and boots. I opted for jeans and a tank top, with my tan blazer thrown on for a professional feel.

We waltz into the restaurant, and I'm worried I won't be able to recognize Natalia. I'd only seen her those few seconds, and I was pretty distracted at the time. She had straight black hair and bright blue eyes. That's all I remember.

We stop at the concierge and tell him we're expected. He leads us outside to the garden villa, as he calls it. It's quiet and soothing, a few tables filled with early lunch-goers. We turn a corner, following the concierge to Natalia when I stop in my tracks.

Two tables away.

Staring at a phone with a plate of ravioli in front of him.

Devon.

I keep walking.

Maddie grabs my elbow, which tells me she's spotted him too. Fortunately, he's turned away from us just enough that I can sneak past without—

Maddie shoves me directly into his lap. I squeal. Devon almost jumps up but sees it's me fast enough that he doesn't send me toppling to the ground.

My first instinct is to strangle him. I want to kick him and yell at him for not rushing off, getting help, and running back to me ready to commit. No, instead he's dining on Italian comfort food, soaking in the California sun.

"Hi," he says.

"Hi."

I stand up and smooth out my jacket as I glare at Maddie. She continues to follow the concierge to a table where a dark-haired girl waits.

"You stalking me?" Devon asks.

I narrow my gaze at him. He's dressed in a button down shirt and jeans. His hair is styled smoothly, and he looks delicious. I push the thoughts of him naked out of my head as I answer. "No. I'm here for a meeting, thank you very much. A meeting you're about to make me late to."

"Then don't let me hold you up." He grabs his fork and digs into his lunch.

I turn to walk off, and immediately regret sounding snappy.

"How have you been?"

He wipes his mouth with a cloth napkin and looks up at me. His eyes evaluate my face and move down lower to my neck and lower to my chest and lower... "Same as usual."

What's that supposed to mean, *same as usual?* Same moody Devon? Same drug-using Devon?

"Have you heard from Lex again?" I want a sign, anything that can mean he's thought about what happened and what'll become of us.

"Nope. I assume she meant it when she said she wanted nothing to do with my family." He gestures toward an empty chair in front of him. "Sit."

I open my mouth to object, but since I'm here to meet with a complete stranger about who-knows-what, I think Natalia can wait. I sit down and look over to Maddie to make sure things are okay over there. I feel bad leaving her to entertain Natalia alone—wait, no I don't. She pushed me into Devon's lap. This is all her doing.

"So," I say.

"So."

My nails dig into my thigh as I try to make sense of all that's changed between us. Who are we now? Do we still have a chance?

"Have you found a job yet?" he asks me.

The blue of his eyes shine in the sunlight, and I find myself mesmerized. Look away. I force my gaze to trail away from his eyes to the scruff on his cheek. Then I'm staring at his lips. Full and pink. Those lips feel so good against my skin. That mouth can do anything, from bringing me such intense pleasure to causing me so much pain.

I take a deep breath. I did the right thing by walking out on him. It's clear we don't hate each other—I could never hate him, but he took me seriously. I just have to give it time now.

"No, I haven't found a job yet. I haven't been looking that hard though, and I still have those voicemails from random event people calling me. I'll get ahold of them.

What about you?" *Have you stopped doing drugs yet?* "Things going alright for you?"

"Yeah. I'm just, you know, living day-by-day." He looks around. "Hey, you want to get out of here?"

"What? No. I already told you. I have a meeting." Which I should really get to.

"You were serious about that?"

Oh my god. Did he really think I was following him? "Yeah, I was serious." I shake my head and stand up. "I'm glad you're doing well."

"I'd be doing better if I saw you more."

Devon stands up, moving in close to me. Now there's that familiar scent of his cologne that makes me want to melt into him.

"I told you things needed to...change," I say. I second-guess every word, wanting to give in and let him take me somewhere, anywhere. But I can't do that. "Call me when you're ready to take that next step."

I step around him and resist the urge to look back as I walk over to Maddie and Natalia. As I get closer, Natalia stands up.

"Olivia, hey!" She gives me a loose hug. "Thank you so much for meeting with me. If you need to talk to Devon, though, it's fine. I don't mind waiting. Your friend Maddie is so sweet, and—"

"We're done." I say it with too much force, and it sounds harsh in my own ears. "We're done talking, that is." I take a seat at the table with the girls. Picking up the menu, I use it to conceal my face as I peek over the top at Devon in time to see him paying for his meal and getting ready to leave. My heart aches. He's so close. And he still wants me. What the hell am I doing? Does integrity really matter all that much? *Of course it does.*

I pick the first thing I see from the lunch options and set the menu down, focusing instead on the stranger who insisted on meeting with me.

"How do you know my brother?" I want to get right to the point.

Natalia smiles a wide, straight-toothed grin. "It requires a little more explanation than that. Otherwise, I just sound insane."

I look at Maddie, who's equally curious as we both wait for her to tell us what this is all about.

"Well, I work for a nonprofit organization called the YOUTHelp Foundation. We are committed to bringing the issues faced by teenagers into the spotlight: family problems, drug use, bullying, suicide."

I nod slowly, feeling terrified and intrigued by what all this has to do with me.

A server stops by, pouring us water and taking our order. As promised, Natalia requests a bottle of wine before she continues her explanation. "YOUTHelp was founded by the acclaimed Rhyanne Phoenix. That means we have a number of connections to celebrities, investors, and other organizations and we bring in the most support—professional and financial—with our charity galas. Rhyanne tasked me with the job of picking our guests of honor, and I'd like you to be one."

"Me?" This barely makes sense. My mind spins with questions, and I'm trying to pinpoint why the name Rhyanne Phoenix sounds familiar. But one question sticks out above the others. "Why me?"

"Because of what you went through with your brother—"

"And how do you know about him?" Having a stranger mention him...know my story. I clench my jaw tight, ready to defend my family.

"I'm embarrassed to say, but as you know, we had a long bus ride from Oregon back to here. I do a lot of research for the foundation, so when I spotted you on the bus, and you were so nice to me, I ended up doing a string of searches on my computer, learning about you and Devon, and somehow I ended up on an article from five years ago when..."

I don't know whether to be weirded out or humbled. "So you want me to be a guest of honor because my gay brother was bullied to death?" Hearing the words come out of my mouth make my stomach turn. Our server returns to the table with the wine, and he can't pour it fast enough. I snatch my glass and gulp the sweet red merlot. "So what would I be expected to do?"

"Not much at all," Natalia assures me. "We would do a short write-up of your story which would be included in the literature we hand to all the attendees. You might be mentioned in a speech, but you mostly just have to show up and be present."

I check Maddie's reaction. She's been quiet all this time, and now she gives me a reassuring shrug to say I should consider it.

"You said celebrity gala though. I'm not a celebrity."

"You don't think so?" Natalia leans back into her chair. "You've been in the headlines with Devon. You two seem serious. I think the events from your adolescence combined with your very high-profile boyfriend make you a perfect guest of honor. There will be a Stone label artist performing, and Stone Records is one of our biggest sponsors, so really, you're more perfect than any other guest."

My very high-profile boyfriend... I look past Natalia to where Devon had been, only to find his seat empty and a bus boy wiping down the table. I can't ignore the hollowness I feel now that he's gone.

Back to Natalia, I say, "Thank you. But— but I don't think it's a good fit for me."

Natalia sits forward. Her smile is still there, but she looks like she's running through all her thoughts. "I know you've been through a lot. I lost my brother when I was twelve. I can't say we'll ever fully recover from it, but from me to you, honestly, it feels good when I get a chance to honor my brother. I think it would do you good to do the same."

"But you mentioned Devon being the reason Olivia would be a suitable guest of honor," Maddie says. It's obvious she's switched from Observant Maddie to Defensive Maddie. "Are you not aware that Devon and Olivia are no longer—"

"No. It's fine." I kick Maddie under the table. I don't need my personal business being spread around. "Devon and I might not be in town when...when is this gala?"

"This weekend." Natalia sits up straighter, looking more excited. "Saturday."

"Oh. Is that enough time? I mean, I don't have anything to wear. I don't even know what to wear."

"Let me worry about all that. As a guest of honor, your presence is all that's required. You and Devon will be the highlight of the evening."

"Me and Devon?" Maybe I should've let Maddie break that bad news. "Can't I just attend by myself?"

"Why would you want to? You'll be the star. We'll take care of everything you need. You'll have Devon by your side. You'll be doing all this for Jared. Why not make it an incredible night? It'll be like Cinderella, only you have no curfew." She laughs at her own joke while I make a decision.

"Alright. Fine. I'm in."

Natalia grabs her phone as soon as I give my answer and makes a call. I grab my wine just as quickly, draining the last of it.

"It'll be fun," Maddie says quietly, leaning in toward me. "You can do this."

I can. I don't have to worry about what I'll wear or how I'll look. I don't have to worry about the actual events of the evening. I just have to worry about making Devon my date without sending him the wrong signals.

Go with me to this gala, but then we're back on a break.

Be my sexy date, but don't try taking advantage of the situation.

Let's look like we're in love while I feel like we're in love. But we can't be in love...Not yet anyway.

That last one is especially scary. Am I to that point now? I don't want to be without Devon. I want us to make each other better. I want to spend every moment by his side. Am I in love with him?

After I've polished off most of the wine on my own and we've all finished our lunch, Natalia says goodbye, and Maddie and I return to her car. I collapse into the seat feeling like I've just had a root canal rather than a lunch meeting.

"I cannot bring Devon to this gala." I rub my eyes, trying to think up a solution. My thoughts blur into one as my head spins from an unexpected afternoon buzz.

"Why? It's for a good cause. You know he'll go."

"And how can you be so confident?"

"Really? Do I have to point out the obvious denial happening between you two?" She starts the car and heads back to the apartment. "I saw the way he looked at you. You know how thrilled he was when you fell into his lap? You're welcome, by the way."

"No, I'm not grateful for that awkward encounter. You know how tense it was? We couldn't think of anything to say to each other. It's like things might really be over." I watch out the window, barely noticing the buildings and pedestrians. What if it *is* over? I can handle it. There are other men out there.

But I don't want another man. I want him.

Maddie lets out a huff of air. "You two are perfect for each other. For whatever reason, you're both holding back—"

"Because he needs to prove to me he can be a better man. I can't be with someone who hides from reality."

"Mhmm. And you really think this time apart is going to help him improve? He can't fix himself if he sees no purpose."

"Which is why I left. It's why we're on this break to begin with. And it's why I can't just waltz up to him and ask him to go with me to this gala." And she thinks *she* has to point out the obvious.

"One look at you all dressed up for your guest of honor role, and he'll drop to his knees and beg for forgiveness."

I roll my eyes at the ludicrous image.

"Anyway, doesn't it feel weird to be invited alongside other celebrities?"

Luckily, I know Maddie means no harm in this. Anyone else asking so bluntly, and I'd feel insulted. "It's weird, yeah. But it's normal. Like the free cupcake thing. Devon even said it would happen. Being with him will bring all sorts of perks, like job offers and free pastries." I laugh.

"So then you don't have a choice. You have to ask Devon to be your date."

She's right. But I have to do it carefully. I don't want him to think everything's better. Not until he cleans up.

"You think Dr. Shannon can give dating advice?"

Maddie gives me a weird look.

"I have an appointment with her this afternoon. Perfect timing, if you ask me."

CHAPTER THREE

"I want to try something new with you today."
Dr. Shannon sits up straighter in her seat.
Her blond hair is down today and barely
reaches the shoulders of her blue jacket.

I'm too distracted by the events with Natalia to be in the mood for a new experiment.
Everything's been such a whirlwind lately
with Devon and work and all the unanticipat-
ed surprises that have come along the way.
My anxieties and dealing with Jared's loss,
both seem a little distanced and mundane, like
it's an issue someone else is dealing with.

"I want us to try hypnosis."

"Hypnosis?" Is she serious? She's been a great doctor who's taken obvious care in pushing me and helping me cope, but carnival sideshow tricks are definitely not my style. "You're joking, right? Is this today's ice-breaker?"

"Actually, hypnotherapy is a valid technique that can help bring up buried feelings and bring you clarity."

Clarity. Now that seems nice. I raise an eyebrow and shrug. "Alright, if you think it can help, I'll trust you."

She has me lie down on the couch—maybe I'll take a nap instead. I watch as she stands up and reaches toward her desk, pressing a button on a sound machine. The steady clicks of a metronome begin. *Tick, tick, tick.*

"All I want you to do right now is listen to the sound. Focus on each beat and let your mind wander." She continues to talk in a low soothing voice, reminding me to relax and only focus on the sound. *Tick, tick, tick.*

She tells me to close my eyes if I want, but make sure I'm still listening. She tells me if an image pops into my mind, to hold it, evaluate it, see where it takes me. I'm tempted to laugh, but this really is relaxing.

After a minute—or maybe five—the rhythm seems to slow. I can't tell if Dr. Shannon changed it or if it's just because I've been listening long enough, but it feels like all of time has slowed down. The effect is mesmerizing, and as I sink further into this time-warp feeling, an image does appear in my mind.

A hospital bed.

For a second it's empty, but then I see Jared's frail, beaten body covered up to his shoulders in an itchy blanket. He looks like he could be asleep—maybe he is. But he stayed that way for days before he left us for good.

"I'm so sorry Jared." I place a hand on his chest and then find where his hand rests below the blanket. I grip it with my own. He doesn't move.

If I'd been on time. If I'd stuck up for him. If I'd forced my parents to take him seriously.

I'd been so angry with mom and dad after. They denied all the supposed rumors about him being gay. They never stopped to accept Jared for who he was or considered what would've been best for him. They told him to deal with the bullies himself. They argued with the press when they referenced Jared as homosexual. They never did anything before *or* after his death to help him.

Neither had I...

Tick, tick, tick.

And then silence.

I open my eyes. Like a TV being shut off, the memory simply stops.

"When you're ready, I want you to tell me what you saw, if anything. Even if it was silly or seemingly non-consequential. Let's talk about the symbolism and potential meanings behind—"

"I've been blaming my parents for Jared dying in vain. But I'm to blame too." I sit up and rub the back of my neck. "When I was still a teenager, it was easy to think I couldn't make a difference, but I'm an adult now. I can't blame others for my inaction. I don't think I can blame them for my other issues either."

Dr. Shannon nods slowly. "Good, good. This is great, Olivia. Let's dig deeper into these revelations. Want to do another round with the hypnosis?"

It's my choice this time. I could just thank her and leave for the day. But my body feels lighter. I actually feel excited. "Yeah, let's try."

It takes several minutes to find my focus again now that my mind feels awakened. As time slows like it had before, I see a bed again. *Tick, tick.*

This time, Devon's bed.

I'm in my purple dress with my head on his chest. This is that disappointing night after the party at the Stone mansion, when I divulged too much personal information that left me crying instead of kissing him. After he'd comforted me, I stayed there, listening to the sound of his reassuring heartbeat and savoring every rise and fall of his chest. Eventually, I fell asleep, and that was the end of it.

"You're amazing, you know that?" Devon's voice is hardly above a whisper.

I don't remember him saying that, but I feel myself smiling at his words, whether they're a memory or a fantasy.

"You're unpredictable and charming," he confesses as I drift off to sleep. "Stubborn and guarded and undeniably sexy."

I wish I knew whether these words were really his or those I'm making up in my mind right now.

His fingers graze my back in a slow circle. "Are you sleeping?"

I don't answer. *Tick, tick.* If this really happened, I'm certain I'd been too close to falling asleep to be able to speak anyway.

"Good," Devon says, "because I couldn't tell you this otherwise. You aren't like any other woman I've met. You caught me off guard, and now I don't want to let you go. You're the kind of girl I can see myself being with...for good. It's too soon for you to know all this. But from my lips to your sleeping ears, I really hope this works. I'll make sure it does."

Tick. Silence again.

I stare up at the ceiling catching my breath. My cheeks warm at Devon's confessions, and I hold onto every word, hoping it really happened. Even if it wasn't real, my body doesn't seem to know it. My unsteady heartbeat thumps as my veins seem to be pushing fire through my body. Every inch of me wants to run to Devon. Wants to leap onto him and kiss him, to tell him we'll work through it all together.

"When you're ready, let's talk about what you saw."

I nearly forgot I wasn't alone in here.

I take a deep breath and sit up. I let the silence linger as I try to sort through my thoughts. Yes, I want Devon. I won't deny it. But a scene playing out in my head doesn't guarantee he actually feels that way. I need him to prove it. The Devon I've gotten to know over the past couple weeks, he'd stop at nothing to get his way. I just have to be patient. Either he'll come back to me, or he'll make it clear there's no more to us.

I can be patient. It's only a matter of time.

"Are you ready to tell me what you saw?"

I consider being honest, but then say, "It was the same as before. The stuff with Jared." I don't want to psychoanalyze my Devon issues.

She opens her mouth to speak, but hesitates a moment. "Well, I think you should take advantage of your revelation. You're a twenty-two-year-old woman, and as you said, it's up to you to take action. How about you find some time to visit Jared's gravesite? Go to him and say goodbye. Use it as a chance to do something for him, honor him."

"Honor him," I repeat. Natalia comes to mind. "What about a charity gala? Would being a guest of honor, there on his behalf, suffice?"

"That's very bold of you, but simple steps may be best. Organizing an event like that would—"

"It's already been organized. I've been invited to attend. It's meant to honor Jared and others like him, just like you said. The problem is, I'm supposed to have Devon there with me, and with us being apart right now, I just don't know how to make it work."

"Maybe there's someone else you can bring. Someone who shared in your loss, and who understands what all you've gone through." She's looking at me as though this all makes perfect sense.

"Who? My mom? Dad? I haven't spoken to them in years, and I don't think I'm ready to confront them now."

"No, not your parents. Someone else. Who loved Jared too. Who felt his death as deeply and as personally as you did." She waits to see if I put it together. "You should invite Rhys to attend this gala with you."

"Rhys? I haven't heard from him since I moved. I don't know where he is. What he's been up to."

"Sounds like a perfect opportunity to take action. Put in the effort to contact him, and see how it pays off."

Contact Rhys. Contact Jared's first and only boyfriend. The kid I grew up alongside because he was Jared's best friend before he'd become more.

That evening, I sit down at my computer wondering where to look first. Rhys Everton. The Rhys I remember had shaggy blond hair, like he was always returning from surfing. I remember his messy eyebrows that hovered over his dark brown eyes. In middle school, I even had a crush on him, but he and Jared teamed up like annoying little brothers— hogging the living room, playing air guitar in their boxers, making fun of my boyfriends, playing tricks on me—and I quickly got over wanting to date him and instead wanted to punch him.

Rhys Everton, who, one day was a part of the family and the next—after Jared's funeral—wouldn't look any of us in the eye. Even if I found him, what are the chances he'd want to speak to me?

I begin by doing a basic Internet search. Several Rhys Evertons show up, but none appear to be him. I check results in the news section and come across an article written shortly after Jared's death. There's a school photo of Jared with a group of friends, and Rhys is mentioned in the caption. It's like after everything happened, all of us ceased to exist. Our world stopped, and here it was frozen in time.

A knock at my door breaks my concentration.

"You hungry?" It's Maddie. "I'm ordering pizza. That's okay, right?"

When has pizza ever *not* been okay? "Sounds good."

"What's wrong?" She walks into my room and stands behind my chair leaning down to rest her chin on my shoulder. She looks at the photo on my screen. "Your brother?"

"I'm trying to find someone. Dr. Shannon suggested I invite Rhys to the gala. That it would help with closure."

"Who's Rhys?"

"This guy," I say, pointing to the grinning blond in the photo. "Jared's best friend. Boyfriend."

"Wow. Lucky for you it's easy to hunt people down online now."

"You think? This is the only result I've gotten so far, though I'm sure I can find more as I keep looking."

"Get up." Maddie stands straight and pushes on my shoulder. "Get up and let the professional do it."

"Professional what? Snooper?" I laugh.

Maddie takes her place in my seat, and logs into her social media profile. I've avoided those sites. I'm not sure Internet friendships and virtual walls filled with other people's drama would benefit me much.

"Last name?" Maddie clicks on a search window and starts typing.

"Everton."

Search results pop up with a handful of matching names and variations of: Reece, Ryan, Riles, Everman, Evanston, Everly.

She starts clicking through to the ones that match, but the profiles are either set to private with no identifying information or are clearly not the Rhys I once knew.

"I don't know, Maddie. Who's to say he even has an account?"

"Oh ye of little faith. Persistence is key here."

I'm not completely computer illiterate. I can do research and use all the basic software without any hitches, but tracking down human beings? It's just not my thing.

Maddie continues typing and clicking, while I stand behind her feeling useless. The sound of the doorbell is a welcome surprise and gives me something productive to do.

"I've got it."

Assuming it's the pizza man, though I don't remember seeing Maddie finish her order, I swing the door open wide, anticipating the lovely smell of grease and cheese. To my surprise, Natalia waits at my doorstep.

CHAPTER FOUR

"Oh, hey," I say, trying to think of how she'd know my address.

As if she heard me, she starts by saying, "My boss gave me the directions. I hope it's not too late, but I've started planning your agenda and needed to touch base with you."

I step aside to invite her in, and we take a seat on a couch. Maddie emerges from my room balancing my laptop on one hand. She stops when she sees Natalia.

"You have a way with figuring out private information, huh?" She looks to me. "Hey, maybe she can help locate—"

"Nope. No, that's okay." I give her a death stare. I don't want anyone to know who I'm trying to find right now. It's still too weird for me.

"'K. Then I'll just be in here." She nods her head toward her bedroom before retreating to it and shutting the door behind her.

"You have a great friend," Natalia says, pulling a notebook from her purse. "But it must be easy to be your best friend, as nice as you are."

"Thanks." I pick at my fingernails, scraping at bits of polish. "You mentioned an agenda? I thought you said everything would be taken care of?"

"Absolutely. All the work is on us. Don't worry. No, you, my dear, are getting the full star treatment. Dress fittings, jewelry pairing, hair, nails...Hell, I can get a teeth whitening session in if you'd like."

I want to laugh. Is she serious? Am I about to become a human Barbie doll? I'm sure a boutique could donate any dress, and I'd love it. "Is all that necessary?"

Natalia flips her hair behind her shoulder and laughs. "You know? In all my time doing this, I don't think I've ever come across someone who wasn't thrilled to be spoiled."

Spoiled. Alright, fine. It could be fun. It's not like I have other plans this week, and it would certainly take my mind off my feelings for Devon.

"So what first?" Certainly, this all shouldn't be too big of an ordeal.

"Tomorrow morning, you have an appointment with Raul Xavier—he's one of the top stylists of the stars. He'll make your beautiful hair even more beautiful."

Right. "But it won't stay that way through Saturday..."

"Of course not, he's just giving you a cut and dye job tomorrow. He'll be there Saturday, along with Trish Martinez—a fabulous makeup artist—to get you all ready right before the gala."

That thought about all this not being a big ordeal was way off. This is going to be a whole fiasco leading up to the event, isn't it? Still, a little glamour would be a nice break from everything that's been happening.

"O!" Maddie's door flings open. "Liv-ee-uh! I need you in here a moment, please and thank you."

I laugh at her. "I'll be just a second," I tell Natalia, and join Maddie in her room.

Closing the door behind me, I ask, "Did you find him?"

"Yeah." She points at her screen. "I also found *this*." Her voice has an angry tone. Someone's in trouble.

I step closer to find her looking at a photo of Corey, surrounded by two half-naked girls. "What am I looking at, Madd? What did you find about Rhys?"

"Never mind him for a second. I looked for Corey before, but I figured, since he's a little more high-profile than other guys I've dated, it wasn't worth much of a search—he wouldn't have a public account. But then I find this. Look, he's using this ridiculous username, Master VIP, to disguise himself. I only found him because your Rhys happened to be at an event Corey was also at. It's crazy that I even noticed this, but the worst part. Look at when he posted this picture of him with two whores."

I squint and lean in closer. Yesterday.

"Maybe it's old?"

"It's from a party over the weekend, so no...not old."

"Right. I'm sorry, but I have to say it." I step back and sit on the edge of her bed. "You hooked up with the guy at a party. You said you've seen him a couple more times, but are you two more serious than a casual fling? Did you agree to exclusively date each other?"

She sighs. "No. And I really wouldn't care if he saw other people at this point, but he was so quick to post this photo, where are the ones with me and him?"

I try to contain it, but a burst of laughter escapes me anyway. "That's what you're worried about? Why your photos aren't appearing online?"

"It symbolizes way more than that, Liv." Now she's forcing back a smile. "Trust me. This pisses me off."

"Then go kick his ass."

"I should." She stands up. "You know, I will. I was supposed to meet him later tonight anyway. Maybe I'll show up early and surprise him and his girlfriends."

She starts digging through her closet for something, an outfit, shoes, a golf club to hit him with—who knows with Maddie.

"Before you get too sidetracked, can you tell me about Rhys, please?"

She stops what she's doing and comes back to the computer. "Right." She clicks a couple times. "He's right here. And he seems to be doing well for himself."

I move to her desk, sitting down and preparing for whatever I might see.

Rhys Everton

Location: Silicon Valley

Occupation: CEO and Founder of Everton Tech

Relationship Status: Married

Wow. He's all grown up now. When you consider he'd only graduated high school two years ago, making him twenty, he's done far more than I have.

I scan through his photos and feel a sharp pang in my heart. Still with his shaggy blond hair, the photos document his happiness. Pictures of him surrounded by friends, accepting awards, buying a house. An entire album is dedicated to his wedding, and I click inside to see gorgeous photos of him at the alter staring lovingly at his tall, dark, and handsome husband.

I'm happy for him. I truly am. But a part of me can't stop seeing Jared standing there instead. Sure, very few relationships at fifteen last long enough to make it to this point, but without Jared here, and with their relationship cut so short, who knows what could've become of them.

"So what should I do now?" I can't just stare at Rhys through the glass wondering "what ifs" on my brother's behalf.

Maddie clicks a button and my email opens with his address ready to go. The message window taunts me, blank, ready for me to make initial contact.

"Right. I'm really doing this."

"Unless you want me to write it for you?"

I shake my head. "No. I've got it. Besides, you've got a man to set straight."

As I type, I listen to Maddie shuffle around her room, getting ready to go. She puts on a shorter skirt and does her makeup extra smoky and sultry. This is Break-Up Maddie.

She's going to go show him what he'll be missing out on.

I try to keep my message concise and find myself typing and deleting sentences over and over. Finally, I end up with this:

Rhys,

It's Olivia Margot, Jared Margot's sister (but I'm sure you know that). I'd like to talk to you about something. I'll keep it brief, but if you could call me, I'd really appreciate it.

Hope all is well,
Olivia

I finish by typing my phone number and hover the mouse over "Send" as I contemplate whether or not I should be doing this. He moved on with his life. He was doing great. Why bring up past memories? It would only be painful and—

Maddie pushes down my index finger, and the message zooms away through virtual pathways straight to Rhys's computer.

Maddie finishes getting ready with no further comment. I've left Natalia waiting all this time, so I push Rhys from my mind, and return to the living room.

"So sorry that took so long," I tell an empty room. She's not here. Her bag sits on the floor, so she hasn't left. "Natalia?"

She walks out from the direction of my bedroom. "Sorry, I was looking for a bathroom."

"Right there." I point to the closed door near the kitchen.

Maddie walks up behind me. "She can track down your apartment, but she can't find a room with a toilet?"

I elbow her. "Be nice."

"I'm always nice." She gives me a quick hug and slings her purse over her shoulder. "Now, I need to go beat up a boy. I won't be too late."

She leaves and Natalia comes out of the bathroom. Instead of sitting, she picks up her purse as if to leave.

I smile, the adrenaline from finding Rhys settling in. "So hair tomorrow morning. Anything else?"

She pulls a paper from her notebook and hands it to me. "After Raul, you're going to stop by Calypso Day's studio for a dress fitting, and that takes care of Wednesday. Then we don't need you again until Saturday."

I look at the paper she's given me. It's complete with times, locations, and directions.

"Sounds good." I give an encouraging smile, though I'm still pretty sure all this fuss is too much. No one will be paying that much attention to me at the gala.

Natalia gives a little squeal and hugs me. "You're going to have a ton of fun. I swear. Thanks for being so great about all this. Your brother would be proud."

Proud of what, I'm not sure, but Natalia knows more about this event than I do. Surely, it'll do good things for youth all over the country. That's something to be proud of.

"Now first things first." She plops back down on the couch, her notebook in hand.

Apparently, our work here isn't done.

She clicks a pen and pats the cushion next to her. "I'm sorry. This part will be a little difficult. I need you to tell me about the events surrounding Jared Margot's death."

Wow, cutting right to the chase. I sit down, but I'm nowhere near prepared to talk about this.

Dr. Shannon's office. My revelation. We hadn't done anything to help Jared then. Is this my chance to do something now?

For the next hour, she interviews me, asking questions that bring all my nightmares into the spotlight.

What was Jared like before it happened?

Were there any warning signs?

A boulder-sized lump wedges itself in my esophagus as I choke through these answers.

Was anything done to prevent it?

How did he die? When? Where?

By the time she's done, my face is wet with tears. My shaky hands clutch a pillow in my lap, and I can feel myself shutting down. Closing off. I want to run away from it all. Be left alone. But the harsh reality is it would just keep following me.

No, I need to face it. I have to.

It's for a good cause.

Once Natalia leaves, I collapse onto the couch, feeling exhausted like I've just lost a brutal battle. I start to doze off, but my phone rings. I force myself off the couch and into my room where I'd left it charging.

Or I thought I did. It's not on my nightstand, so I must be even more tired than I thought. It rings again, and I follow the sound to my desk. No, not on the desk but laying on the chair instead.

"Hello?" I answer. That reminds me. Maddie never called in that pizza order.

"Olivia?" a male voice responds. "It's me. Rhys."

"Rhys. Hey! Wow, that was quick." My legs shaking, I sit down.

"Yeah, I'm away on business and happened to be wasting time on my phone when your message came through." He sounds just like the Rhys I once knew. "So you wanted to talk?"

"I do. If you have a few minutes now, I can probably—"

"How about we meet up? I'm in LA. Your mom said you live here, right?"

I push my hair behind my ear. His easygoing tone is relaxing and contagious. "I do. If you're busy though—"

"Nonsense. I'm here. You're here. Let's catch up. I'm free all day tomorrow. We can do lunch."

I remember tomorrow's schedule with the salon and Calico Day—or whatever her name was. "I think I can do two o'clock. Does that work?"

"Perfect," he says, sounding excited.

He gives me the name of a diner, and my face almost hurts from smiling as we hang up. I can't wait to see him tomorrow.

And I can't wait any longer for pizza. I place an order, looking forward to eating as much as I can by myself before the celebrity beauty gurus get ahold of me.

CHAPTER FIVE

She sent a limo. I was ready to go, keys in hand, and when I left my apartment, I was greeted with a long white limousine.

We pull up in front of Raul Xavier's right at 9:00 a.m. Today's definitely going to be an interesting one. I check my hair and makeup in my compact mirror. I know I'm about to get it done, but I confess, I spent a little bit of time—like an hour—making sure it looked good going in. If they're really celebrity stylists, I have to compare on some level, right? Otherwise, even I'd be laughing at myself.

Okay, this is it. Olivia's Cinderella fairy tale begins now. My fairy godmother, Natalia, told me not to be late, so I stop wasting time and go to the salon's front door. I pull. It doesn't budge.

The damn thing is locked, and a closer look at the engraved text on the door tells me they don't open for another two hours.

What the hell, Natalia?

Maybe I got the time wrong. It's possible. The agenda is in my purse, so I dig into my bag to find it.

"Olivia?" a voice calls. "Uh—I mean, Ms. Margot."

I look back up toward the salon to find the door open wide, a flustered girl holding her chest as if to catch her breath.

"I am so sorry," she says, pausing between each word. "I was expecting you, and I was on my way over. I can't believe I made you wait. I'm so, so sorry."

Why would she be apologizing to me? Last time I went to a salon, I waited well over forty-five minutes before my stylist got to me. This was nothing.

"It's okay, really. I saw you open at eleven. I can come back."

The girl gives a shriek of laughter like this is comedy hour. "You're hilarious. You have a private appointment. You're the whole reason we're here, and it's truly an honor. Now come in."

She steps aside and extends an arm as if presenting me with my grand prize. I walk in expecting the usual—reception desk, waiting room chairs, and a dozen huge mirrors paired with salon chairs. What I find is extraordinary. The waiting area is a lounge, complete with plush couches and a bar. There's no reception desk, and a silky drape separates the waiting area from the stylist stations. I take a peek past to see it's one big room with only one chair in the middle. One wall is completely lined with mirrors. How this place stays in business only serving one client at a time, I have no idea. Oh wait, celebrities. They can afford the steep pricing, and therefore, Raul must be making a fortune. Good for him.

"Can I get you a drink? Mimosa? Champagne? Cucumber water?" The girl heads toward the bar.

"A water, I guess."

She works quickly and hands me a glass. "I'm Vivian, by the way. So sorry to not introduce myself already."

"No need to apologize, Vivian. I'm Olivia."

"Of course you are. We're thrilled to have you here today." She beams a toothy grin, and I still can't understand why she's so excited to see me.

I sip at my refreshing, cool water and watch little slices of cucumber float around on top. Music plays from invisible speakers, pumping out electronica at a pleasant volume. If I forgot about the real purpose of this place, I could easily convince myself I was at the most peaceful nightclub. I'd be a guest every night at a hangout with this atmosphere.

"Raul's ready when you are, Ms. Margot."

"Please, call me Olivia."

I follow Vivian past the drapes and am met by a man in a black suit. He's suave and dressed for a black tie event, but I'm most drawn to his hair. A mohawk extends a good six inches above his head, and it's dyed a deep purple. I love this guy already.

"Beautiful, Olivia. It is indeed an honor." He does a half bow and holds out his arm for me to take.

I loop mine through his elbow and he leads me to his chair.

A couple hours later, Raul spins me toward the mirror, my first time seeing the final result. When I said I tried to make my hair look nice before coming here, I shouldn't have bothered. Wow. I look like a different person. He's dyed it a deep espresso shade, added natural extensions to give it more volume, and given me these huge, soft waves. I'm reminded of models in magazines that have perfect hair, every strand seeming to know where it belongs. It all feels so bouncy and light, yet there's so much of it!

"Wow, Raul. You're a god with those scissors."

"I am, aren't I?" He polishes his sheers with a square of cloth and returns them to his breast pocket. "You look as beautiful as ever, and I believe I'll see you Saturday. I'll give you a killer up-do, okay sweetheart?"

I stand up and hug him. I can't help myself. I love my hair.

"You're very welcome," he says. "Vivian will walk you out. Take good care of the mane."

I walk alongside Vivian and realize I should probably tip him or something, right?

"What do I owe you for all this?" I ask her.

She laughs that giddy, shrill giggle of hers. "It's all prepaid, tip and all—and a very generous tip at that." She opens the door to escort me out. "It was a pleasure meeting you. We hope to see you again."

I return to the limo feeling like I'd just spent a weekend at a spa retreat. It's noon, and I'm expected at Calypso Day's studio in thirty minutes. Lunch with Rhys is at two, so I really hope this is all over by then. Only...I don't want this star treatment to end. My confidence is already soaring and I've only had my hair done. Now I get to go see my dress. If you asked me a year ago, I never would've predicted this. I'm not sure I would've even been interested in all this glitz and spotlight. But I'm embracing it. And I have to admit, loving it. Who have I become?

Calypso's studio ends up being nearby, and the limo drops me right at the front door. This time, I knock instead of assuming I'll get in. I'm quickly learning things run very differently in the Hollywood world. The door opens and I'm greeted by a slim woman with long black hair that belongs on a goddess.

"Olivia, finally!" she says.

Am I late? I'm about to apologize and explain why it took so long, but she interrupts my thoughts.

"I've been so anxious waiting all morning for our appointment. I already have great ideas for your gown." She says this with her eyes wide and bright. "You ready to get started?"

"You must be Calypso Day?"

She rubs the sparkling stud in her left nostril and opens the door wider to let me in. "I am. But you can call me Caly like all my friends."

So we're automatic friends. Okay, I can use a friend who makes fancy dresses. Her excitement is contagious, and I'm just as eager to see what she has for me.

I go in expecting the same luxury as the salon. Again, I'm taken by surprise. It's a big studio with wood floors and exposed ceiling beams. It's rustic and simple, and it's also a mess. Everywhere I look are racks of garment bags, tables piled high with fabrics and catalogs. Every inch of space seems to be filled with supplies and finished products. Only one corner of the studio is clear of clutter. Under a window sits a single meditation cushion and a small table topped with burning incense.

"Don't mind the chaos. I assure you, I know where everything is. Organization and me? We broke up a long time ago."

No kidding. Maddie would love this place. I'm always suggesting her life would be easier if she straightened up her things. Her argument is always to challenge me. "Name something," she'll say. "Anything, and I'll tell you where it is."

A half dozen people scramble around the studio working as Calypso—Caly—leads me toward the center where a tall mirror stands before a short round stool.

"Please, step up."

I do so and find myself again mesmerized by my hair. It sounds superficial, I know, but I was told to embrace the glamour.

"Cheryl, bring me my samples," she calls to one of the tables. I don't see anyone there until a woman steps out from behind a tall stack of folded silk in deep shades of blue and red and purple. Caly even knows where her associates are hidden. I stifle a laugh at how crazy this place is. But you can't help but be intrigued by it all.

Cheryl hands Caly what looks like a fat, oversized binder. Instead of papers and sheet protectors, rectangles of fabric make up the contents. Caly flips through as if looking for just the right page. Occasionally, she stops and pulls out one of the colors. After a couple minutes, she has about twenty layers of fabric draped on one shoulder. She pulls a pencil from her back pocket, hands the sample book back to Cheryl, and grabs a sketchbook.

"I was under the impression you were doing a regular dress fitting," I say, letting my curiosity get to me. "Like an already finished dress?"

"Oh hell no," Caly shouts. "Olivia Margot is *not* getting a pre-made. You're going to that gala with a custom as every celebrity should."

"That's very kind of you, but I'm no celebrity. They're making me out to be a big deal, and I mostly feel like a sham."

"I've been there," she says, shaking her head and smiling. She begins holding different pieces of cloth up to my face. When she speaks again, she goes a mile a minute, seeming to never stop for a breath. "This fabric is exclusively mine. It's elite quality, sent to me directly by my private manufacturers, and is my best kept secret. This is how I'm going to make it big in the industry. Other designers? They're begging to find out what I'm doing that's so different from them. All I do is laugh, because when it comes to it, those other designers are creating what the masses want and expect. I not only think outside the box, I've *banned* the box from being anywhere near me. They need to realize it's all about creativity and—oh my god, this is it!"

She's holding an icy blue satin to my face. She moves down, holding it over my shoulder. She rests it on my breasts, letting it go and analyzing the way it lays over my curves. This entire charade is almost comical, but I'm getting the impression that I'm truly watching an artist at work right now.

"What do you think?" she asks me.

"Oh, I really know nothing about this stuff."

"Well I know one thing. You are gonna be hot. That's with a capital H." She turns her focus to her sketchbook and I watch as lines and curves, swirls and scribbles transform into an illustrated version of me—fancy hair and all—donning a one-strap, full length ball gown. Her plans show it trailing behind me with a short train, and the whole thing hugs my curves as if the satin has been poured over my body.

"That looks great."

"Oh this. This is nothing, just a first draft. The final product—now that will blow your mind."

She digs into her pockets looking for something but not finding it. Wandering to a table, she scoops up a few books and dumps them onto a nearby shelf. Then she pushes paper and boxes and empty coffee mugs aside until she snatches something in her hand with an "aha".

Caly comes back to me, opening her hand and revealing a tape measure. Mumbling to herself, she takes my measurements and scribbles them onto her sketch. When she finishes, she holds out a hand for me to take. Helping me off the raised platform, she pulls me into a hug.

"Thank you so much for coming by. I promise, I won't disappoint."

I'm still so caught off guard by everyone's reactions today. What happened while I was sleeping last night? Was a memo sent out informing the LA population that I was now some sort of big deal? Why didn't I receive one?

"Oh, before you go, can I ask a huge favor?" Caly rushes to one of the many clothes racks, sifts through it, and pulls down one of the garment bags. She swivels around to another rack, finding two more bags and adding them to the first. She comes back to me, dumps these into my arms, and before I can ask what's going on, she sprints to a far table and comes back with a fabric covered box, like the old hat boxes all our grandma's used to have.

"This is all unreleased product from my new line. Can you take it home, check it out, and consider trying on the things you like?"

Really? "Oh, you're way too generous. You don't have to do this for me. The gown you design will be well enough."

"No, no. I need you wearing these. It'll help my career. I've gotten lucky so far getting one of my gowns featured on an attendee at the HIT Awards." She turns away as if looking off into the distance. "Of course, that one ended up destroyed..." She looks back at me with big pleading eyes. "Please don't destroy these your first time wearing them. But do enjoy them."

"I don't know what to say. Thank you. Of course I'll take them." Never mind my pitiful wardrobe at home. She doesn't need to know how uncool I really am.

I start to pry open the box when Caly shoves it back shut. "Oh, don't open them yet. I love surprising people with surprises. Check them out after you leave." She gives a little squeal and hugs me again before leading me to the door and holding it for me.

I dump everything into the back seat of the limo and pull my phone from my purse. Crap. I definitely don't have enough time to get home, grab my car, and get to Rhys. My driver assures me he's in no hurry, so I tell him where to take me next. I could get used to this.

CHAPTER SIX

I arrive at Colin's Diner a few minutes after two. Several round tables with big umbrellas are scattered around a front patio, intertwined with randomly placed pots of colorful flowers. A propped open door invites hungry patrons inside, but I don't have to go that far. I spot Rhys before I have both legs out of the limo. He stares down at a menu, and for a moment, I'm convinced I've gone back in time. But then he looks up, and the grown up Rhys makes eye contact. I close the door behind me and walk toward him. The California sun has left him tan, and no doubt a gym membership has left him toned. The scruff on his face suggests he's down-to-Earth while his button down and shined shoes say he's professional. The shaggy mop on his head appears to be the only thing he's kept all these years.

"Well well, Miss Hollywood. It's good to see you." He stands up and comes around the table to give me a big hug. "Look at you. If I had to describe the Olivia I thought I'd be meeting here today, I would've assumed she'd have blue hair and a hundred piercings. I would never have expected this supermodel arriving in her limo."

Should I tell him about the salon trip and how the limo is unexpected? Nah. I feel too good right now.

"You're sweet, but I was just coming from something. I assure you, I'm not usually this put together."

He motions for me to sit, and we both take our places. "Well, if I was in any way attract- ed to girls, Devon would need to watch out."

I let out a laugh. "So, since you're into guys, should I be the one watching out in- stead?"

"Ooh, do you think I'd really have a chance with him?"

I playfully kick him under the table. "Oh stop. I'm not here to talk about him."

We order drinks and lunch and continue to catch up. This is actually pretty great. He's the first person from my past I've seen in years. I haven't heard from my parents in months, and even then it's a short phone call here or a half-assed email there. I'm not sure how Rhys felt about me and my family after we lost Jared, but it seems like things could be better now—like a little part of my past has healed.

"So married man. Congratulations, by the way."

He bows his head as if accepting an award. "Thank you. Christopher and I are very happy. I started a software company a year and a half ago, Everton Tech. Christopher was an intern at the time."

"He was promoted pretty fast I take it?"

"You could say that. Intern to spouse in one year, one month, and five days, to be exact."

My heart swoons at him knowing the exact number of days. I let him talk about Christopher as long as he wants, living vicariously through his young, happy marriage. I'm almost in a daze wondering how drastically things would be different if it were Devon and I who married at twenty years old. I'm yanked from this awkward contemplation when Rhys turns the attention on me.

"So tell me about you. It's obvious you've done a lot in a few short years. How'd you get to this point?"

I wave my hand to erase the very idea. "No, no. I—I'm an unemployed college grad." I laugh. Our food arrives. "In fact, I really don't know what's going on right now. In fact, the celebrity mirage I seem to be displaying is partly why I asked to talk to you."

"Now I'm truly intrigued."

"Um...it also has to do with Jared."

The mood of the entire patio seems to dull at the sound of his name. A flood of memories sweeps over our table, and Rhys and I give each other a reassuring half-smile. We've both been in this dark place. We both understand.

"The way I look. My current mode of transportation. Someone thinks I'm more important than I really am. Like I'm a star or—"

"Look, Hollywood," Rhys cuts in, between bites of his club sandwich. "You're dating someone who was once referred to as American royalty. If he's a prince, and you're dating him, that makes you a..."

"A princess...or duchess or whatever. This is all too weird for me. It really is. Anyway, there's a charity gala on Saturday being put on by the YOUTHelp Foundation. I've been invited as a guest of honor, and I know you probably have to get back home soon, but I wanted to see if you'd come along." I shrug my shoulders to make it clear it's no big deal if he can't. I'd be disappointed though. I'd like more time to catch up with him.

"You want me to be your date?"

"Not exactly. I'm supposed to bring Devon as well." I take a bite of my sandwich and almost choke as he answers.

"So you want me to be yours and Devon's date? Nice."

"You're ridiculous. Bring Christopher. I'd like to meet him."

"I think we can work that out. Send me all the details, and we'll meet you there."

"Perfect. Now, tell me—"

Click.

The all too familiar sound makes me lose my train of thought.

Rhys looks past me and down the sidewalk. "I think you have company."

"How many?"

Rhys picks up his glass of water and peeks over the rim nonchalantly as he takes a sip. "I see three."

I groan. "Sorry. They show up out of no-where—their cameras nosing around my business. I can't imagine what it's like for *real* celebrities."

"I have an idea." Rhys sets down his water and leans in closer. "You want to give them a show?"

"Do you not know me at all? Of course, I don't. I want them to disappear and leave me alone. It's bad enough they're going to make up rumors about us now."

"That's my point."

I raise an eyebrow. Apparently, I've missed something entirely.

Rhys stands up and offers me his hand. I hesitate, then take it. He yanks me up to my feet and wraps his free arm around my waist.

"My darling, Olivia." He projects his voice unnaturally and with a misplaced accent to be sure the paps hear him loud and clear. "Be mine forever."

And with that, he bends me back in a dramatic dip and plants a big, sloppy kiss on my cheek near my mouth. From this angle, the cameras would make it look like we're making out. It's so ridiculous. He straightens us back up, and I smack him in the chest, laughing hysterically.

"Oh my god. You just made their day."

Rhys sits back down and goes back to eating as if nothing happened. "It's kind of fun screwing with them. We should hang out more often."

I smooth out my clothes and sit. I feel my phone vibrating in my purse and pull it out to see who's calling. It's Natalia. I apologize to Rhys as I answer.

"This is awful, Olivia. We're having a major catastrophe right now."

She sounds like she's in an empty room, her voice echoing against the walls.

"Okay. What's wrong?" And why call me?

"We're supposed to film a TV spot tomorrow for YOUTHelp. It's this mix of real-life
stories and sponsorship name-drops to en-
courage more donations after the gala. Nolan
Aries was all set to film it. He's stuck in New
York right now working on film pre-
production or something. He was scheduled
to fly back tonight, and now he can't because
of some executive meeting, which means I
have no one to put in front of the camera, unless you'll agree to do it. Please, please,
please."

"You want me to go on TV?" Is she out of
her mind? I gulp my water as I try to think up
the perfect excuse not to. Rhys overheard me
and now his interest is piqued too.

He mouths the word, "TV?"

I move the phone away from my mouth to
respond to him. "No way in hell." I return the
receiver to my ear and listen as Natalia continues to beg and tell me how easy it'll be.

"I'm sorry, Natalia. That's just not a good idea. Don't you have another guest of honor who can fill the spot?"

"Nolan was the best option, period. You're the second best."

Great, second best. I want to laugh, but she's freaking serious about me going on TV. Um, no thank you.

Rhys nudges my foot under the table. "Do it. Come on."

I shake my head no, and he snatches the phone from my grasp. "Hello, Natalia is it? This is Mr. Everton, Olivia's personal life advisor. She'd love to do the TV spot ... yep ... okay, ten o'clock? ... Sounds great. She'll see you then ... What's that? ... Mhmm ... Yeah, she's definitely taken care of that ... Great ... No, thank *you*." He hangs up.

"What did you just do? I can't go in front of a camera."

He hands me back my phone. "Oh please, you just pounced on me and made out with me in front of three cameras."

"You're insane." I'm having trouble feeling the anxiety with him making me laugh. "If I look like a fool, I'm coming after you."

"You'll be fine. You're meeting her Friday at Coastal View High School at 10:00 a.m. Don't be late. Oh, and she asked to confirm you'd talked to Devon and everything was all set for Saturday, which, of course, I told her you've got it all taken care of."

My jaw hangs open for a moment before I snap my mouth closed. I clench my teeth. Yeah, I've totally got that taken care of. Other than seeing Devon, talking to him, and asking him. Dammit, I need to meet with him. I can't put it off any longer.

When Rhys and I finally say goodbye, I feel like I'm parting with a treasured piece of my past.

"I'll see you soon, right?" I say.

"Saturday. We'll be there. It'll be great."

He gives me a long hug, and I see my temporary driver pull up. I turn to leave, but Rhys stops me.

"Hey, Hollywood." He stares for a moment as if he's trying to form the words before he can say them. "I miss him too."

I hurry to the limo before I can start crying.

CHAPTER SEVEN

The problem with taking a complex, secret route to Devon's condo one time is now I don't know where he actually lives. I want to get it over with, but the best I can do is send him a text message and wait for him to tell me where and when we can talk. I have to swallow my pride as I type each word, but the gala is for a good cause. We can both act like mature adults for one evening. It doesn't mean I've completely forgiven him, and it doesn't mean we're back together for good. It's one night, two people, some Hollywood glamour, and loved ones being honored. He'll understand the boundaries, I'm sure.

I have the limo driver drop me back off at the apartment, and I practically fall through the front door, the garment bags and linen box from Caly's studio throwing me off balance.

"Whoa there." Maddie jumps up from the couch to help me. "What is all this?" She takes everything from my arms, and then almost drops everything anyway. "And look at *you*. You look amazing."

She dumps it all onto a couch, and I drop down next to the pile. "I've had...a day."

"I can see that." She runs her fingers over one of my curls. "This is photo shoot quality."

I laugh and push her hand away. "It's no big deal. My hair had to be done for Saturday. And I went to a dress fitting. Calypso Day is making me a gown as we speak."

"Calypso? Seriously? She's like *the* predicted up-and-comer right now."

"She implied that." I point at the stack of things next to me. "She sent me home stuff from her new line asking me to wear it."

Maddie looks at me wide eyed. "All those times I've let you borrow my clothes, you're aware I will be hijacking these from you, right?"

"You're more than welcome to, you know that."

"I do. Now are you ready for the unveiling?" she sings.

"Be my guest." I'm exhausted. My heavy eyes want nothing more than a nap, but Maddie's squeals of approval awaken my curiosity.

She's pulled the lid from the round box and is holding up a pair of fingerless gloves embellished with tiny beads.

"These are amazing."

She sets them aside and pulls out delicate headbands in earth tone colors, colorful scarves meant for fashion not function, and a sexy, studded belt.

"You've hit the jackpot, woman." She turns to the bags next. Unzipping the first, we find that it doesn't hold one, but several blouses and chic tops. Caly has no idea the favor she's done for me. How could I pay her back? A thank you note clearly does not suffice.

My phone alerts me to an incoming message.

Mark's out front. See you soon.

Devon sent his driver to get me? A simple time and place would've been more than enough. And the blunt message. What am I supposed to make of that?

"I have to go meet Devon. Tell him about the gala and all."

She opens another bag and looks through it. "Before you go, change into this."

Maddie pulls out a sleeveless dress with a short, asymmetrical skirt. It's intricate white lace, layered over a skin tone silk. Casual yet undeniably sexy. Devon will love it, but it could only sabotage the message I'm trying to relay. Oh, what the hell? It's really cute.

I change into it and leave, meeting Mark in the parking lot.

"Nice to see you again," he calls to me in the backseat.

"You too. Thank you for chauffeuring me around...again."

About twenty minutes later, Mark pulls up in front of Beauchamp Towers, an insanely ritzy hotel. I am so underdressed. Why would Devon pick this place?

"He'll meet you in the bar," Mark tells me.

"Thanks." A valet attendant opens the door for me, and I step out, trying to gather some confidence.

I walk into a large, marble foyer and marvel at the luxury. Straight ahead, double doors stand open as several employees haul wooden chairs inside. Next to the door a sign reads YOUTHelp Foundation and my heart skips a beat. This is where the gala will be?

How beautiful. To the right, another door leads into the hotel lounge. I'm guessing this is the bar where I'll meet Devon. As I get closer, I spot him through the windows. He sits in a tall stool across from a bartender—both men laughing. A shock sweeps through me at the sight of him smiling, looking so at-ease and happy in a t-shirt and jeans. His dark hair is perfectly disheveled, and he's clean-shaven—did he do that for me? A pint of beer sits before him, and he glances down at his watch. His gaze goes from the time to the door. He's waiting for me.

When he sees me, he freezes in place. Hell, all of time freezes with it. His eyes lock on mine, and the lust behind his gaze sends a chill down my spine. The intensity of it hypnotizes me, the hairs on the back of my neck stand up. There's too much distance between us.

I grab the door handle and open it. Let's do this.

I walk in, and Devon stands up. He takes his beer and approaches me.

"Hi," I say. "Thank you for—"

"Shh." He holds a finger up to tell me to wait a moment. His eyes take me in, scanning me from head to toe. He walks in a circle around me, evaluating me. My cheeks warm, and I hope no one in here is watching this awkward display. Devon completes his rotation and stands close to me. "You look incredible."

I giggle and look down. "Thanks. I had to meet up with people to get ready for the gala. They did all this." I emphasize the "this" with a long hand motion from my hair to my hips, which gets Devon to check me out again.

His interest in me is a relief. He wants me. What will he do to get me?

Devon's hand swipes a strand of my curled hair behind my ear. "Why don't you find us a seat, and I'll get you a drink?"

I head to a quiet corner and sit down. Devon follows a couple minutes later, setting down a bright pink drink in front of me. Instead of taking the other bench across the booth, he sits close to me on the one side. I'm reminded of our first meetings and the way the touch of our hips made me giddy like a schoolgirl. Even now, the few layers of fabric separating us, I have to resist the urge to scoot closer.

I need to get right to the point and not let these feelings linger too long. "I need you to be my boyfriend."

A wide grin spreads across Devon's face. I could've worded that better. My entire intention was to avoid sending the wrong mess—

His mouth crushes into mine, his tongue plunging in and dancing with my own. I'm overtaken by his taste. His smell. His hand finds my face, and I nuzzle against it. The other combs through my hair and grips my neck from behind.

When he pulls away, I gasp to catch my breath. "No. I'm sorry. Let me try again." This time, I explain the gala and how I'm a guest of honor—*we're* guests of honor, since it was made clear we needed to be a package deal.

"So you need me to *act* like your date?" Devon asks, sounding slightly disappointed, slightly amused.

"I need you to *be* my date. Things aren't over between us. At least, I hope they aren't. We can still be a couple, but...well, you know. We have some work to do."

"Then why not take your gay buddy?"

"My what?" Oh yeah, Rhys. The tabloids. The fake kiss. The paparazzi work fast. "Wait. How do you know he's gay?"

"Please, after all the times I've kissed you. That angle would probably land my lips right..." Instead of saying it, or pointing or something, he leans over and kisses that same spot to the side of my mouth. His kiss is much more genuine than Rhys's theatrics, and goose bumps rise along my skin. "Plus, you were laughing. If a random guy really kissed you, you'd probably beat the crap out of him."

"I'm glad *you* saw through it." Imagine how he would've reacted if he'd believed it was real. "But again, how'd you know he's gay?"

"Because if a straight guy had an opportunity to kiss you, he'd do it right."

My cheeks warm and I shift my gaze to the cherry floating in my cocktail. "So...will you go with me to the gala?"

"On one condition."

I raise an eyebrow. There's always something in it for Devon. What does he want this time? His sly grin tells me it won't just be agreeing to a dance.

"We have a penthouse in this hotel. It's pretty great."

Mhmm. I'm sure it is.

"After the gala. I want you to go with me up there."

See? Always making trouble.

He continues, "Just you..." He covers my hand with his own and traces a line on my skin from my middle knuckle to my wrist. I clench my fist to contain a shiver. "And me... The night of the gala. I want us to—"

"Okay, stop. Come on. You know where we left things. It's not really appropriate to—"

"To talk? Damn, Olivia. That's all I was going to say. I want us to *talk*." He drinks from his beer. "You have such a dirty mind," he tells me, his eyes narrowed to imply he knows exactly how that all came across, and it's how he meant it.

"I'm the dirty one. Yes, I can agree to *talking*. I think it'll be good timing. Plus, we'll both be all dressed up. What better for a serious talk than to have two people who look great?" His subtle jokes are way better, but I still laugh at my own.

"You always look great. Dress or," he runs his fingers under the fabric of my straps, my shoulder tingling from his touch. He lifts the

strap away from my skin just enough to make
it feel naked, "no dress."

THIRD DEGREE

CHAPTER EIGHT

The last time I stepped foot in a high school was my final day of senior year. When I walked out of that hallway, I left it all behind. The school. The people. The entire town. You could say I was running away. But I couldn't breathe there. I couldn't face the same small town people day-after-day, so when I got my chance, I fled. Even my parents grew distant as I moved away to start my own life. Weekly phone calls turned into holiday calls. Then the holiday conversations gave way to yearly birthday calls. Now, a rare email was all that

103

kept us in touch, filled with synthetic niceties and exaggerated happiness. According to those messages, the entire Margot family was doing fantastic. New jobs, advanced opportunities, great relationships, and the charade went on and on.

So you could say walking into Coastal View High School on a busy Friday morning to shoot a television spot for YOUTHelp was a little more than surreal. They'd opted to film in the middle of a school day and had releases signed for all the students. Unlike filing with an artificial background or empty school, Natalia explained how this would be more personal, more realistic.

I convinced Maddie to come with me for moral support. Well, we all know Maddie. She didn't take much convincing at all.

"I have to be filmed for a TV thing, can you co—"

"Oh, I'm there! Think I can get in the shot?"

She and I walking into the main hall, it's just like traveling back in time. The clusters of students. The incoherent medley of a hundred conversations going on at once. The lockers and backpacks and binders. For a second, I forget how old I am and feel the slight panic of not knowing where my next class is.

We step into the office to sign in as visitors and find Natalia waiting for us.

"My girl!" She rushes to my side and embraces me in a hug. "You look gorgeous."

She doesn't acknowledge Maddie at all, which is weird. Then again, I didn't ask permission for Maddie to come. And Natalia's job is to focus on me.

"If you're ready, you can follow me to the gym."

Natalia leads us to the other end of the long hallway. A few eyes turn toward us, but for the most part, we're not attracting any attention. We aren't recognizable, and I'm almost tempted to use it as an argument to not go through with this entire thing. *Natalia, notice how no one knows me. You don't want me to be the spokesperson for this public service announcement.*

But I follow quietly as though she's an administrator leading me to detention.

We get to the gym doors, when I hear my name called out behind me. There goes my point about no one knowing me. Maddie and Natalia continue inside as I turn around...and it's like the sea of bodies have parted to make way for a person who definitely *is* recognizable.

Devon's walking toward me. Dressed in an untucked gray button down and dark jeans, every eye is on him. He plasters on his red carpet smile as he accepts hugs from squealing teenage girls and nods toward those too shy to approach him. It's like a bizarre movie moment when the dreamy guy finally admits his feelings for the nerdy girl in front of the whole school. If that makes me the nerdy girl, I accept the title with honor.

Once he's close enough, I ask, "What are you doing here?"

He shakes someone's hand and continues toward me, placing a hand on each of my shoulders. "If I know anything about you, it's that you're freaking out right now. So I came to—"

"Take my place? Oh please do!"

He laughs. "No way. You're going to do this. I know you can."

"Fine. But if I know anything about you, it's that you hate all this attention." I nod toward all the students behind him, still staring our way.

"You know me very well. But it's a small price to pay to make sure you don't run away from this."

"Oh thanks."

He kisses the top of my head and ushers me into the gym. Inside, lights are set up at different angles, illuminating a tall stool sitting under a fat microphone. Two cameras are set up, pointed at the stool, and another is on wheels off to the side, focused on nothing specific. I turn to take in the chaos of the setup crew and spot Maddie heading my way. I look around for Natalia—knowing I should formerly introduce her to Devon—but she's nowhere to be found.

"Where's...?" I start, but Maddie looks flustered. "Everything okay?"

"Yeah. Fine. Your wrangler said she had to grab something."

"Are you referring to me as livestock?"

She laughs, and the unexplained darkness in her mood lifts away.

"Ms. Margot. If you don't mind, we need you in makeup," a quiet voice says to my right.

The voice belongs to a short, round woman who's had a little too much plastic surgery. Her makeup is caked on, and I'm worried she's going to do the same to me. I let her lead me to a corner that's partitioned off by tall curtains. Inside, it looks just like a little dressing room. A vanity is set up covered in trays and bottles of makeup and hair products. A big mirror surrounded in lights makes the entire space bright. A rack of clothes waits to one side where another crewmember is sifting through the options. He's taller and in a suit with a measuring tape draped around his neck like it's a fashion accessory.

"Drake, Ms. Margot is ready." The woman pats me on the shoulder and then leaves the makeshift room.

Drake turns around, takes a moment to evaluate me, and then grabs two hangers in a very decisive manner. "Put these on. I'll be back in one minute."

He leaves as abruptly as he speaks, and I survey the outfit he's handed me. A slightly low-cut, dark green top and a pair of khaki dress pants. I change into them both, relieved it's nothing more...glitzy. Checking myself in the mirror, I can tell this outfit is meant to send a mix of signals. The collar and buttons on the top make me look casual, even professional, but the low neckline should draw in the eyes of men who prefer to be persuaded by means other than words and facts. I look like I could be attending a business meeting, giving a presentation, or strolling along the beach. The versatility of this outfit is almost fascinating.

Drake pops back in exactly sixty seconds after he left. He briskly walks to the rack and retrieves a thick belt, some jewelry, and a pair of heels. He works fast but doesn't speak, looping the belt around my midsection over my shirt, clasping a gold necklace around my neck, and places the heels at my feet for me to step into. I can't tell if he's rude or focused, but I kind of appreciate the quiet.

As a final touch, he flicks open the top button of my shirt, revealing a decent amount of cleavage. Once more, he takes me in from head to toe and then, "Roz," his voice bellows through the silence and the woman returns. "Makeup."

He walks out again. Roz smiles to me and motions toward the chair in front of the mirror. After a few minutes, and a surprisingly light touch, Roz has my skin glowing, my eyes bright, and my whole face camera ready.

"Thank you," I say. My voice is starting to tremble. This is becoming very real.

Back out at the lights and cameras and...*set*, that's what it is, I take a deep breath. Maddie and Devon stand off to the side having their own conversation. They look up as I appear and give me encouraging smiles. Maddie adds in a big thumbs up.

A man in a black t-shirt and torn jeans, carrying a clipboard waves me over. He gets me positioned on the stool, my back turned to the bleachers. He checks a camera and has me pivot more to the right. He adjusts the camera angle to bring a basketball hoop into the background of the shot. Another crewmember comes over to me and holds a small box to my face.

"What is that?" I ask.

"Light meter. Make sure you look perfec-to!"

Roz comes up next with a powder brush, dusting my face across my forehead and down my nose.

As I sit there—my only job right now—other people come up to me, one after another, like they've lined up to do so, to fix my hair, adjust my shirt, move a light.

When the fiasco is over, someone goes to the gym door, opening it wide. In small clusters, high school students enter the gym, stopping at the doorway to receive instructions, and then making their way to their designated marks.

Some end up on the bleachers behind me. Others are directed to stand in casual conversations on the gym floor. Others are told to enter or exit from another door behind me. I try to picture all this from the camera's perspective. I'll be front and center, and behind me, it'll be like school's in session—a totally natural occurrence. Completely and undeniably "natural".

I bounce my leg and squeeze my hands together, tempted to wipe the gathering layer of sweat onto my pants. An unnamed crewmember comes over with a towel. She hands it to me with a kind smile, and I try not to look like a fool drying my hands.

"Here," she says. "A trick I like to use." She pulls a bottle from her pocket and squirts a white lotion onto my hand. "Rub them together."

As I do, the scent of peppermint drifts upward. I breathe in the soothing smell and feel my entire body relax a little.

"It's got essential oils in it, and the lotion itself dries into a sheer powder that'll help keep those nervous palms under control."

She turns and walks back to her spot. I want to thank her, my anonymous heroine. Feeling a little more calm, I watch as the man with the clipboard holds a hand up. The crew falls silent. The students fall silent.

"Once we're rolling," he says, "my extras know what to do. Remember the blocking we practiced yesterday. And Olivia, you'll simply read off the cue cards. Ready?"

"Mhmm." Or not at all. Just read off the cue cards. *Simple.*

"And...rolling... Action."

It was anything but simple. After six takes, I'd stumbled over every line at least once, and I almost toppled off the stool while acting "natural".

After the last "Cut!" the director says, "Let's take five and try again."

I exhale a breath I hadn't known I was holding and stand up to stretch my legs. I close my eyes and remind myself to calm down. When I open them, Devon fills my view.

"You're doing great," he says.

"I don't like liars."

He smiles and runs a hand through his messy hair. "Fine. You're a little...new to this. But you'll get it."

"It's that stupid line I have to say about Jared. *My younger brother was a victim of bullying. He died in a school much like the one I'm in now.* He was attacked in the woods. He *died* in a hospital. It's not...I don't know...It's not accurate."

Devon takes my hands in his and brings them up to his face, kissing them. "I know it's rough. And it's true it's not going to be factual. It's Hollywood. They want investors, donations, attention. Don't think about the parts that are wrong. Think about the good it'll do." He drops my hands and lifts my chin. "Think of the good *you* are doing."

With that, he gives me a quick kiss on my lips. It's over too soon, but I know what he was doing. There are invisible boundaries between us right now. He's being careful not to cross them.

But since I'm the one who made them...

I reach around his neck and pull him back to me. My mouth collides with his, and I kiss him with all the emotion I can put into it. I close my eyes to soak him in. He smells like comfort. He tastes like adventure. His arms find my waist and draw me closer. The rest of the world disappears.

Well, not entirely.

My concentration is broken by the sound of dozens of high schoolers hooting and hollering and whistling as they cheer us on.

I break away from him, my cheeks burning from the attention of a room packed with hormonal adolescents.

The director asks if I'm ready for another take, and I nod. I sit back down, and Roz comes over to touch up my makeup—mostly my lips.

Two takes later and it's done. I can't say I'm proud. I'm sure ninety percent of the footage filmed today is a wreck. But they're the professionals, and when they said, "That's a wrap," there's no way I was going to argue.

I get up and accept another kiss from Devon. This time, the high schoolers disperse and there's no embarrassing cheering. I savor

Devon's tasty lips, but then I'm caught off guard by a raised voice out in the hall.

Maddie.

She's visible through the open door. I watch as she raises both hands to accentuate some point. I can't make out what she's saying, but by her face, it's obvious she's angry.

"I'll be right back, okay?" I tell Devon, removing my hands from his warm chest.

I leave the gym the way I came in. Now I see Maddie's in the middle of berating Natalia.

"Hey, hey!" I step between them. "What's going on?"

I look from Maddie's enraged face to Natalia's big smile. "We're fine, Olivia. Just having a discussion about some—"

"No. Don't even try to play it off like it's nothing." Maddie looks like she could strangle the girl, but after everything Natalia's done for me and what she's working so hard to do for my brother and others who suffered the same treatment... I can't let this stand.

"Maddie! I asked you to come because I knew you'd support me. I knew you'd be excited about all this. You can't be attacking the people I work with. This is supposed to be a professional environment. We need to be mature." The look of surprise is startling, like I've just betrayed her, so I follow with an apology. "I know you probably mean well, but—"

She puts her hands on her hips. "You know what? You're right. This is your business, not mine, so I'll stay out of it. In fact, I'll wait in the car until you're done."

"You don't have to do that. I—"

"Oh no, it's fine. I don't want to mess up the professional atmosphere of a *high school*. But you might want to ask your boss here if you'll be needing to write your speech yourself or if they'll have a professional write the words for you."

"What are you talking about?" I turn to Natalia, who's frozen in place.

Behind me Maddie makes one final argument. "I'm starting to see through your bullshit," she tells Natalia. "It's only a matter of time before Olivia sees it too." She stomps down the hall, which is now much emptier than before. Unlike the schools you see on TV, these students actually attend class.

"I wanted to let you know how great you were in there." Natalia is still grinning ear to ear. Had she even heard Maddie? No wonder my best friend got so mad. She clearly wasn't getting through to Natalia, and nothing infuriates her more than not winning an argument.

"What was she talking about, Natalia?"

"It's no big deal. We're working on the final plans for the gala, and were thinking a quick five-to-ten minute speech would be great from you."

"Whoa. That's not what we agreed on." I look down the hall in time to see the school doors close behind Maddie.

"I know it wasn't in the original agree-ment, but really," she laughs, "neither was this shoot, and you did fabulous. Now you're kind of the face of this whole thing, so wouldn't it be great for you to get up there on the big night?" She pats my shoulder. "You know, be the star?"

It makes sense, doesn't it? And I guess if I can get in front of the cameras, then—but I don't—it's not what we agreed to. Dammit. I shouldn't have been rude to Maddie. If she were here, she'd have my back....And she had. That's what the whole argument was about. I'm an ass. Now I'm going to be in over my head.

"So what do you say? We can help you pre-pare. We can even have it written for you by an experienced speech writer."

"Yeah...I mean, I guess that's—"

"Great! You'll be perfect. Let me make a few calls." She turns on her heel and walks toward a connecting hall. The magical lotion must have worn off because my palms are damp and my heart is racing. No, no, no. I can't do this. It's not me. It would go horribly wrong.

"Wait," I shout. "Natalia. Stop."

She turns back with the same plastered smile. How long has she practiced that?

"I can't. I mean," I try to sound firm. "I won't."

She walks back toward me, and I catch a subtle huff as she gets nearer. "Of course you can."

"No. And it's not up for discussion. We agreed I'd attend the gala. I specifically said I couldn't be involved more than that, and yes, I went ahead with the TV thing, but that's it. I'll be at the gala Saturday. Devon will be with me. I'll fulfill my end of the bargain, but I'm not available to do more beyond that. Okay?"

I hold my breath waiting for her rebuttal. I don't have much argument in me, but if my options are to speak up now or on a stage in front of tons of guests, I can take on my one-woman audience.

"Okay," is all she says.

I wait for more. Looking away, I catch a glimpse of Devon walking toward me. He could stand up for me, though I think I'm doing an okay job myself.

Her smile's faded, and when she spots Devon she snaps her focus back to me. "You're right. I'm sorry I was going to push for more. I'll see you Saturday. It'll be fine. Friends?"

"Of course."

She gives me a quick hug and leaves to get back to work.

Devon comes out and stands behind me, wrapping his arms around my shoulders. He speaks low into my ear. "Everything alright?"

Mmm. Definitely, now that I have him this close. "Everything's fine." Actually, it's pretty great. I stood up for myself. I got the result I needed. One point to Olivia! Maddie would be proud.

Oh shit, Maddie.

"I gotta go." I turn around and kiss Devon quickly. "Maddie's waiting in the car. I'll see you Saturday."

CHAPTER NINE

The good news is, I got to take home my camera debut outfit. The bad news is, Maddie was silent the whole ride home.

We go into the quiet apartment, and before Maddie can retreat to her room, I say, "I'm sorry, okay?"

She stops in her doorway and looks back at me. "It kind of sucks you defended Natalia without hesitation, when I'm your best friend. The one who knows you better than anyone else. The one who knows there's no way in hell you'd stand up in front of a crowd and talk about Jared."

"You're right. I'm an asshole. And I'm sorry. I told Natalia no, though. She tried to convince me it would be the right thing, and I held my ground. I said no."

"Good." She turns to go in her room, and pauses again. Without looking back at me, she says, "I'm proud of you, you know? You've come a long way in a short time. Standing up to Keenly. Standing up to Devon. Now Natalia. Hell, even me." She laughs. "My girl's growing up."

I smile. She's right. I have been more vocal lately. I've felt different too—like I've gained confidence and found my own strength. And I know what stubborn sexy man to thank for that.

Devon.

My phone's buzzing on my nightstand in my pitch-black room. It's got to be eleven or twelve at night. I look closer.

1:00 a.m.

And it's Devon calling. Something must be horribly wrong. I fumble with the device as I hit the button to answer it. I clumsily sit up in bed and mumble a, "Hello."

"Hey baby. I'm right out front. How about you let me in?"

It doesn't even sound like him. I mean, it's his voice. That sexy gruff is unmistakable. But if it wasn't for that, I'd think someone stole his phone and was playing a prank.

"You're here?" I need a mirror. No way am I presentable right now. My hair's in a high, crooked ponytail, and I'm wearing only an oversized t-shirt.

"Come see for yourself," his voice teases me and I hear a quiet tap at my front door.

Holy shit. He's really just stopping by in the middle of the night. I scramble out of bed, my phone still pressed to my ear. I click on a lamp, pull my ponytail down, and comb my fingers through my hair, all the time telling Devon, "I'll be right out ... I'm on my way." I check my face in a mirror and wipe at my smudged eyeliner. I should know better than to go to bed without cleaning all my makeup off. "One more second," I tell Devon.

Finally, I check my breath and spray myself with a quick mist of perfume. I swear I'm not over doing it. I just...okay, I'm over doing it.

"Alright," I whisper into the receiver. "All ready."

I sneak through the living room, hoping to not wake Maddie. Since ditching Corey, she's been taking extra shifts at the bar the past couple nights, determined to make enough money to do something else with her life—her words, not mine.

I reach for the doorknob, still talking to Devon on the phone. "But what are you thinking—"

I open the door, and sudden paralysis sends my phone toppling to the floor. The thump of it snaps me out of my shock. "Devon? What the hell?"

He stands there, one arm gripping the doorframe to support him upright. A layer of sweat covers his body. His shirt is all disheveled, along with his hair. And his eyes... The pupils are so large, it's like I'm facing a wolf in the dead of the night.

"There's my beautiful girl," he slurs. "Get dressed. Go back in there." He points into my apartment while walking in at the same time, his body following his pointing finger. "Go back in here and get dressed. You. Me. We're going out."

His voice carries across the silent apartment. I hush him while pulling him into my room. "Maddie's asleep. What are you doing here?"

I get him into my room and shut the door. He hurries to my desk shuffling things around. "You should change." He lifts up some papers and looks behind books in quick, jittery movements. He looks like a paranoid schizophrenic searching for proof he's being watched by the government. His words come out in excited fragments. "You waiting for? Going out. Come on."

"No Devon. We're not. Are you...? What are you on?"

He laughs and moves to my closet. "A little whisky. A little white." White? Does he mean...He sniffs and continues, "More in my car if you want to try." Shuffling through my clothes, he starts pulling down shirts and skirts and a winter coat that's completely in-appropriate in this California climate.

Before he disrupts everything on a hanger, I grab his arm and pull him away. Dammit. So much for any hope of him changing during this time we've been apart. I can't believe he came over here high. And that he wants me to do drugs with him? Has he completely lost it?

As I pull him to the center of the room, far from any more of my belongings, he hits the edge of my mattress and falls into my bed. "Ooh. Like the way you think. Come here, beauty queen." He pulls me down on top of him and kisses me hard on the mouth. My head swirls. Minutes ago I was fast asleep. Now I'm on Devon. If it weren't for his current frame of mind, I could almost think this was the beginning of a fantastic dream. But the reality is, he's high on fucking cocaine, and I have no idea what to do with him. What do I do about this?

I savor the taste of his lips for a brief moment before pulling back. "How about *you* stay right there and get some rest. Sleep it off."

"I want to sleep you off."

What the hell does that even mean? He grabs for my hand, but I step back. He's staring up at me, and as long as he's keeping his mouth shut, I could easily stand here and stare back until the sun rises.

"I know it's you," he says.

He's still not making any sense.

I sigh and sit at the edge of the bed. "What?"

"The phone calls. You've been trying to reach me." He shifts toward the headboard of my bed, propping himself up. "Calling me. Just to hear my voice. All hours of the day and night." His icy gaze meets my bewildered one. "You miss me," he says.

I do. I know I do. But it's *this* version of him—this is what I can't handle. But...I haven't been calling him. Staring at my phone, considering it, yes. But not calling him.

"I don't know what you're talking about. I haven't—"

"Your phone calls." He reaches into his back pocket and retrieves his phone. "I'll show you."

Call me confused. I watch as he swipes and scrolls. Then he holds his phone out. "See. My proof."

A row of unknown calls is sandwiched between two calls to Kaidan.

"My calls would have my name, Devon."

"Not when you're being all secretive. That's why I..." Like he's been distracted, his voice trails off and he stares toward the window. I follow his gaze, but there's nothing there.

What the hell's wrong with him? He's talking nonsense. He looks pale and sickly. Should I be worried? Of course I am. But I don't know what to do with this. Drug use? Maybe an overdose? I hold back the urge to scream.

Maddie could help, but I'd feel like a jerk waking her. No, I'm an adult. I can deal with this. I have one idea. I snatch his phone out of his hand. "You stay here. Give me a second."

I take his phone out into the kitchen, and before I can lose my confidence, I call Kaidan.

After a few rings and expecting his voice mail, I hear, "What the fuck do you want now, Devon?"

"Um...I'm sorry. It's actually Olivia. Uh— Olivia Margot, Devon's—"

"Yeah. I know who you are. What do you need?" He pauses. "And sorry for the way I answered."

I take a breath and tell him everything as fast as possible. "I don't know what to do. I saw he talked to you recently, and since he's your brother—"

"Oh shit. Did he get himself killed?" He sucks in a breath.

"No, no. He just—um—he showed up at my apartment. He's really high or drunk...or both. I don't know. It might be an emergency or...I don't know what to do, Kaidan. Am I supposed to take him to the hospital or something?"

I hear him expel a held breath and let out a relieved laugh. "No. Toss his ass on a couch, and he'll sleep it off. Typical Devon is all. This is the sort of bullshit he pulled in high school and he's right back at it..." A muffled noise implies he's pulled the phone away. I hear his voice in the distance talking to someone else. Then he's back in our conversation. "He'll be fine, Olivia. It's good you're taking care of him."

"Right. Okay." More relaxed, I thank him and hang up.

Back in my room, Devon's passed out sleeping in the middle of my bed.

Oh Devon. We've got to figure this out.

We.

Would he be in this state if I'd been with him? If I'd forgiven him? If I want him, I have to accept all of him. That's all there is to it.

And I do want him.

He's not off the hook, but maybe...like me, he just can't heal alone.

I walk over and remove his shoes, placing them on the floor. I turn the lamp off and slip into bed next to him. One hand on his chest, his racing heart worries me. But he's here. I can watch over him.

He'll be okay.

CHAPTER TEN

It's the morning of the gala, and Devon's gone before I wake up. My half empty bed leaves me wondering whether he was there at all. I'm certain I hadn't dreamt of him showing up high as a kite and acting like a fool. Plus my pillow smells like him. I close my eyes and breathe him in.

I miss him. I'll stay here a few more minutes until the scent of him fades away, but then I'm getting up and doing something with myself. It's an important day. I should go to the gym...if my membership is still active. Or maybe get a massage. Or...

"Olivia. You have guests," Maddie calls from my closed door.

I open my eyes to blinding sunlight. My arm's draped across the pillow that smells like Devon—only now it doesn't anymore. Guess it's time to get up and start my day.

I look at the time on my phone.

Noon! Holy shit. I fell back to sleep for hours.

I leap out of bed and rush to my door, throwing it open. "Hey," I say to Maddie.

"You have a...a crew here. Were you asleep?"

A crew? I grab a pair of jeans hanging on the back of my desk chair and jump into them. Grabbing a random shirt from my closet, I toss it over my head, dressing myself as quickly as possible. I can't believe I slept half the day away. And *today* of all days.

"Can you stall them? Please?"

I don't even know who "them" is, but I need two minutes to make myself not look like a mess. I don't wait for an answer from Maddie and instead, head to the bathroom where I brush my hair and my teeth. I clean my face and add some moisturizer.

There, now I look a little more...awake.

Noon. Damn.

I walk out into the living room and stop short. My "crew" has taken over my entire living room, seemingly filling every inch of space.

Calypso Day and that girl, Cheryl, from her studio, wait next to a tall trunk on wheels. Raul Xavier sits on the edge of our couch, hands in lap, looking pretty uncomfortable. And Natalia stands off to the side with someone I don't recognize—must be Trish Martinez, the makeup artist she'd mentioned. Trish holds an oversized makeup case, so it's obvious all my gala prep will be done right here, in the Margot-Lowell residence. I'm reminded of circus performers packed into a clown car. Our tiny living room barely holds everyone, and the stiff looks on some of their faces makes it clear they, too, were expecting more from the guest of honor.

Maddie turns around from her spot on the love seat. "They're all ready when you are. I think we can move the kitchen table to the side and have more room."

I look from one end of the apartment to the other. I'm such a fraud, and all these people now know it.

After Maddie and I move furniture, we try to get some order figured out. Natalia dons her personal assistant role and begins listing the agenda and timeframe of each step.

Dress.

Hair.

Nails.

Makeup.

And the catered food will arrive in two hours.

All this? For me?

"Go on, rock star. Get all done up." Maddie pushes my shoulder while I stand here idly wondering when was the last time I dusted. Does the trash need to be taken out?

We've never had this many people in the apartment and especially nobody with Hollywood high standards.

Calypso gets things rolling by shoving her trunk across the living room and positioning it in the middle of the clear space we've made. Her assistant unlocks the giant box and pulls out a small round stool. Calypso—Caly— motions for me to come over. She hands me a small garment bag and tells me to go change into its contents.

Before I retreat to my room, I turn toward our apartment guests. "You know, my best friend Maddie here is also attending the gala tonight. I'd appreciate it if you gave her the same formal treatment I'm getting."

After all, she's just as "famous" as I am.

In my room, I open the little garment bag to find a lacy white corset top and a sheer thong. These are extra hot, but how am I going to squeeze into this corset on my—

A knock on my door, followed by it opening and Caly coming in. "Cute right? That'll make your boobs look fab. And the underwear is to make sure you have no lines. It'll just look like you're naked under the gown."

Naked. Awesome. I fight the temptation to make a sarcastic comment. I know Caly worked hard on my dress. She knows better than I do what underwear is required for it.

She helps me into the corset. It's surprisingly comfortable in its formfitting magic. I change into the thong and try to ignore how exposed I feel.

"Let's see how the dress looks."

I don't move. My apartment is packed with people and she wants me to walk out there like this?

Caly puts a hand on her hip before spotting my fuzzy bathrobe. She throws it at me. "You know how many naked people we've all seen? It's no big deal, especially not in fashion."

She turns and I follow her out feeling too much like a prude. Caly leads me to the short stool and motions for me to step onto it. Maddie sits in a chair with Raul behind her. He's equipped with a curling wand and giving Maddie's blond locks their own makeover. Trish stains Maddie's lips a deep red and touches up the smoky eye shadow that makes her eyes stand out brilliantly.

Caly's looking at me grinning from ear to ear. "You ready for the big reveal?"

Of course I am. Her mockup sketch had me drooling over the elegance and luxury of it. And she promised the final product would be even better.

Cheryl pulls down a much larger garment bag and unzips it.

"Wait!" Caly stops everything and rummages through one of her bags pulling out a silk scarf. "Let me blindfold you."

Um, okay. "Sure."

Her excitement fills the little empty space left in the room as she ties the fabric around my head, blocking out everything.

Next thing I know, I feel the robe being removed. My cheeks warm and I'm certain they're bright red. At least with the blindfold on, I can convince myself no one's looking at my half-naked body.

Fortunately, these girls work fast and I feel soft, heavy fabric slip over my head and hug my body. A few tugs and a zip later, all hands are off me. I hear Caly gasp.

"Yes," she says in an affirmative tone as if someone just asked a doctor if the surgery had been successful.

"Damn girl," I hear Cheryl say. "You've done it again."

Hello? I'm still blind here and now I'm dying to see what they're seeing. Somebody reaches up and unties the scarf. It slides away right as Caly pulls the door of the trunk open wider. It's lined with a full-length mirror, and the reflection I see is extraordinary.

The one shoulder strap is embellished with lace and tiny Swarovski beads. A loop of icy blue fabric slips off my shoulder in a seductive way. It catches the eye and sends it looking down to the satin bodice that hugs my curves in the most flattering way. My god is it sexy, while still looking appropriate for the charity gala. The train adds a dramatic touch while a thigh-high slit makes sure the bottom of the gown is just as tantalizing as the top.

And this was all made for me.

I hold a hand to my mouth. "Caly. Thank you. You went way beyond what you needed to for me."

"It's perfect for you," she corrects me. "And since there aren't any issues, your friend can wear your back up gown."

"You made me a second gown too?"

"Not exactly. I always design a couple others out just in case Plan A doesn't work out. I technically made you three. But since Number One is glamorous, the other two become back stock for others who need something."

What she's saying is, she designed three gowns for me. And the extras could be worn by other celebrities. I can just picture an award-wining actress walking down the red carpet wearing a Calypso Day designed for Olivia Margot...Yes, this is getting way beyond weird.

Caly continues, "So Maddie, you have your pick." And with that she pulls out two more gowns. One is all white, lacy, elegant, and stunning. The other is a sexy red gown with practically no back to it. Maddie snatches the gorgeous crimson dress with a, "Ooh. Hell yeah," and races to her room to change into it.

I laugh and Natalia ushers me to my next spot. She's pulled out a dining chair for me to sit, so I do as I'm told. These people aren't my crew. They're my fairy godparents dressing me up for a royal ball. It's made more obvious by what they place on the table before me.

Three boxes lined in black velvet display the biggest, most blindingly bright diamonds

I've ever seen. I know I sound like an idiot, but I have to ask. "Are these real?"

I get a couple raised eyebrows and no further response. *Of course they are, O.* Caly lifts a sparkling necklace from the box and fastens it around my neck. This thing is heavy! I check it out in a smaller mirror. Princess cut diamonds line my neckline and cascade down to my cleavage. I'm mesmerized by their ability to look delicate yet bold.

While I sit there trying to calculate how much this one piece of jewelry must be worth, Caly sorts through the other two boxes—both containing a variety of earrings in all shapes and sizes.

"You're giving her an up-do right?" Caly asks without turning around.

Raul responds from behind us, "Yes. A few tendrils will be loose, but her ears will be mostly visible."

"Let's keep it simple then." I'm not sure if she directs that at me or Raul. But she sifts through a few more styles before picking a pair of flawless studs. Then she cruelly takes all my jewelry from me and passes me off to Raul. "We don't want him snagging something with a comb, now do we?"

Raul gives a little "humph" before spreading out his supplies on the same table. Meanwhile, Maddie's door opens, and out walks my beautiful roommate. She gives her best impression of a model on a runway, striking dramatic poses. "Please tell me there are some killer shoes to go with this."

Caly prances over, eager to complete another gala ensemble. "I'm going to have Olivia wear these lower heels, because something tells me she'll be more comfortable with them."

"I'm right here, you know."

But the girls laugh at my lack of balance, and Calypso pulls out a pair of studded black stilettos. They look like a murder weapon—a fashionable, statement-making murder weapon. Maddie practically leaps into them.

An hour later, I have my hair twisted in intricate spirals in the back of my head. It's intentionally messy with the few tendrils he'd mentioned framing my face.

"Ooh." Caly looks at me for a long minute while Trish works on my makeup. Caly goes to her trunk and opens a few more boxes. She's fit so much stuff in there, it's like she played a game of Tetris to pack it.

When she walks back to me, she holds a diamond-encrusted comb. It's shaped like a large feather with strands of sparkling diamonds hanging from it at different lengths. She and Raul fumble with placing it in my hair. When it's just right, they pull their hands back with a synchronized "aha". Now my up-do is complete with even more sparkle.

I'm grateful my makeup is done in a way that looks natural and subtle. Everything else is so over-the-top, I can barely recognize myself. They finish me off by replacing my jewelry and helping me into my heels.

Standing next to Maddie, we check each other out as our fashion crew evaluates their final products—smoothing stray hairs and brushing across our faces with powder. When they're happy, the apartment settles into a peaceful quiet.

"You two look like fire and ice," Calypso remarks. "Stellar."

CHAPTER ELEVEN

Silence. That's the reaction I get when I open the door a couple hours later for Devon. Catering came and went. Maddie and I were carefully hand fed while a nail technician gave us manicures to complement the rest of our look. Soon after, everyone packed up and left. My cramped apartment expanded the instant it was vacated. We had enough time to breathe a sigh of relief before the doorbell rang announcing the arrival of my date.

Now I stand in the open doorway looking at Devon looking at me. He takes in my hair, my jewelry, my gown—particularly the long sexy slit up the thigh—and it takes him a moment before he speaks.

"And I thought I'd found myself the perfect simple girl."

"I'm not sure how to take that." Is simple a good thing or bad here?

He moves closer to me, and I step backward inside. "Any Hollywood starlet would look dull and ordinary next to you. There are no words for how beautiful you look."

I could stand here and let him continue showering me with compliments. Instead I clutch his flawlessly pressed white dress shirt in one fist and pull him closer to me, kissing him. Devon in a tux is gorgeous. Devon in a tux while lavishly praising me is irresistible. My lips collide with his, and his arms find the bare skin on my back. His palms pressed against me, his arms secured around me...I could stay here forever.

But then I remember Maddie's in the room. I pull away feeling rude. She stands off to the side staring into the kitchen.

"Sorry," I say and clear my throat. Back at Devon, I ask, "Where'd you go this morning?"

From the corner of my eye, Maddie perks up. I forgot she wasn't aware he was here last night—not that it was all that exciting.

"Family drama." Devon smooths his hair and straightens his tuxedo jacket. "For once it had nothing to do with me."

"Good..." Not sure I want to know what other issues his family is having. I think it's normal for them. "We ready to go? Mark out there?"

"Actually, I'm driving tonight." Devon jiggles his keys for emphasis. "Thought it would be better if it's just you and me."

But Maddie needs a ride I'm sure. I'd feel awful making her go by herself. As soon as I turn her way and open my mouth to protest, she speaks up. "I have a ride tonight. Don't worry about me."

"Are you sure?"

"Absolutely. I'm riding with my hot date."

Hot date? She hadn't mentioned bringing anyone. I'm glad my guest list was unlimited, and now I'm curious what new guy she's got in her life.

I grab the clutch Caly assigned to me featuring similar embellishments as my gown, toss in my phone, and give Maddie a quick hug. "I'll see you soon, then."

Devon leads me out to his Camaro and opens the passenger door for me. "Oh wait." He pushes past me and leans into the car, pulling out a giant bouquet of white roses. Handing them to me, he speaks sincerely. "I need to apologize for last night. A lot happened. I shouldn't have shown up here and brought you into my mess."

I'm glad he did. I want him to know he can rely on me. But seeing him like that... I can't demand that he change for me. I just have to hope he'll do it for himself.

"Thank you, for these. I think we can talk about the rest later tonight."

He spreads his lips as if readying to say more, but stops and motions for me to get in the car instead. "Let's not be late to your big event."

The first time I came to Beauchamp Towers, it was like any other ridiculously nice hotel. Valet greeted guests out front. The hotel was pristine and inviting. Everyone seemed friendly.

But tonight it's transformed into a secured location exclusive to only those select, important people. The front entrance is closed off by metal barriers. Backdrops featuring logos for YOUTHelp, Stone Records, and others sponsors span one wall, and a red carpet leads the way to the front doors. We pull around to the side where valet waits. They open the doors, welcoming us, and take the car while Devon and I proceed to the guest entrance.

"You've never walked a red carpet before." Devon holds my hand tighter. "You don't have to say anything. Just keep your head up."

And don't trip.

First, we're greeted by staff wearing earpieces and holding clipboards. "Good evening Mr. Stone and Ms. Margot." How awesome, we didn't have to tell them who we are.

As I step onto the famous red carpet walkway, the aura of importance seems to wash over me. I don't necessarily feel more confident, but just having people treat me like I'm *somebody* is beyond my wildest dreams. Soak it all in. This fifteen minutes of fame is bound to run out at some point.

Devon does the honors of shining his brilliant smile at the media. He wraps an arm around my waist. "Smile for the cameras," he mumbles through gritted teeth. "And imagine doing this hundreds of times."

It must get old quick, but I love him for sucking it up and playing his celebrity part for me.

We stop for another camera, and I look up at Devon in time to catch him checking me out instead of looking out at the crowd.

"Hey." I give him my best flirty smile. "Thank you."

He leans down and kisses me. A whistle from the crowd makes me want to rush through the rest of this slow walk inside.

The next camera flashes and a Hollywood news reporter asks Devon about recent rumors revolving around the Stone family.

"Aside from being a sponsor, Stone Records is completely irrelevant tonight. This is Olivia's night, and it's all about the YOUTHelp Foundation. Let's focus on that."

His smile and self-assurance don't waver as he firmly turns them down. I'm in awe by the power behind his voice. This is how the Stone family gets whatever they need. It's all about their confidence and the sense of authority they take on when they're in the spotlight.

Finally we get inside and the party is in full swing before us. We don't make it six steps before we're crowded by others.

A guy in a gray tux with slicked back brown hair grabs Devon's hand shaking it enthusiastically. "Devon. Great to see you here. How are you? Kaidan? I heard—"

"We're good. This is Olivia." He presses his hand to my back in a gesture meant to bring focus to me while making it clear I'm his.

He continues to boast about me and talk about the gala, while diverting all attention off him. As we make our way through the quickly filling room, I notice just how many celebrities are present. *The* R&B superstar Bia says hi to us, and Devon introduces me to the guests that accompany her—Ethan Beckham and Zoe North. Ethan, I recognize, and hold back a laugh as I remember Maddie should be here soon. She's going to freak. Zoe, on the other hand, I don't know, but according to Devon, we'll all know her very well soon. The fiery redhead is determined to make her second big break after a former stint as a child star. As we talk, I remind myself tonight, I'm just like them. We're all here for the same purpose, and no matter how out of place I am, Devon is making sure everyone leaves knowing my name. It takes me a while to accept what's happening here. Devon Stone is acting like the perfect gentleman.

We find our table, and I sit down, taking in the scenery while Devon finds us something to drink. Everything is done up in creams and purples to reflect the YOUTHelp logo. The table's centerpieces are simple flower arrangements of white roses and lilies, and next to them a large wooden placard showcases photos of victims—young kids and teenagers who went through what Jared experienced. I spin the surprisingly heavy placard around to the other side and find my own brother's face staring back at me. A punch to my gut that I can't fully process as Natalia swoops in beside me and sits down in Devon's seat.

"You look...phenomenal."

I knew Jared would come up a lot tonight. I clench my fists, swallow the pain, and focus on what's important.

I smile at Natalia. "Thank you. And thanks," I look around the grand room, "for all of this."

"Oh please, my job was to wrangle you here. The planners and event committees—and Rhyanne, of course, they're the ones to thank. Speaking of, come meet her. I've told her all about you."

Natalia pulls me from my chair, and I follow hoping Devon gets back quickly with a strong drink. We weave through the crowds moving toward a stage until we're face to face with a tall, classy-looking woman wearing a black strapless gown with elbow length gloves.

"Rhyanne, this is Olivia Margot. Famous girlfriend of Devon Stone and my favorite guest of honor tonight. Olivia, this is Rhyanne Phoenix, my beautiful, wonderful boss."

Rhyanne's gloved hand shakes mine. "Natalia here is always a charmer. It's a pleasure to meet you."

Rhyanne's presence is dominating. She has a certain grace and authority about her, which makes sense being the president of a nonprofit that dishes out harsh truth and advocates for a misunderstood minority. I know her though. Rhyanne Phoenix isn't just a nonprofit founder, she's an actress. And not just an actress, she's best known for being the first transgender woman to be cast in a lead role in a network drama. The show she was on won all sorts of awards and lasted for ten seasons. I'm an idiot for not remembering her name before now, but seeing her, I'm suddenly far more excited about everything that's been going on, as well as everything to come. Rhyanne is someone who can get things done.

"It's an honor to meet you." I'm holding back a maniacal grin. I want to hug her. Instead, I try to keep it cool. "Natalia's been great this week. It's incredible how much was accomplished in such a short time."

We make small talk for another minute before Rhyanne's pulled aside by an associate. I thank Natalia again for choosing me and make my way back to Devon. He's standing by our table talking to other guests. When he spots me, he holds his arm out to embrace me and hands me a glass of wine that I graciously accept. Tonight's perfect, and if this is part of the Hollywood life, it's easily my favorite. All that's missing now is for—

"Olivia," sings a voice from behind me. Maddie's here.

I turn to find her arm-in-arm with her date—correction: dates. On her left, his shaggy blond hair smoothed out nicely, is Rhys. And on her right, a man in a gray suit with piercing dark eyes. He smiles, and one of the photos from their wedding crosses my mind. Maddie's dates are Rhys and Christopher.

I rush over and hug all three of them— never mind that I haven't been officially introduced to Rhys's husband. I love them all so much right now just for being here.

"Hope you don't mind, but I hacked into your email and got Rhys's information. I told them I needed a ride, and they showed up with a stretch limo. I like their style." She's still holding onto their arms, and I notice she's a little wobbly.

"Have you been drinking Maddie?"

"I like their style *and* their limo's champagne selection. I need to be a part of this Hollywood thing. The glamour, the parties. Didn't you love that red carpet walk in? That was, like, the real deal. And the photos will be awesome—me and these two hunks—holy shit!" She lowers her voice to an exaggerated whisper. "Ethan Beckham. Fifty steps away. Excuse me."

"Maddie wait." I hate to disappoint her, but Ethan's hand was securely fastened to Zoe North's hip earlier. I'm pretty sure he's not available tonight.

"I'll be right back. I gotta go work my magic."

She'll figure it out soon enough.

"She needs a boyfriend," Rhys says.

"You're telling me." The poor girl has been dating all the wrong guys. I wish she'd find someone perfect for her. But she'll end up with several more Ethan-types—arrogant, selfish, disloyal—before she gives up on that type and finds someone good for her.

But who am I to talk?

Devon pulls my seat out for me, and we all take our places at the table. I finish my first glass of wine and accept another. Maybe a buzz is sinking in, but I look at Devon and can't pull my eyes away. The smooth skin lining his jaw. The pale pink of his lips and the glint of his teeth as he cracks a joke, to which Rhys and Chris burst into laughter. His icy eyes glance over to me and seem to stare straight into my soul. Our eyes locked, time slows. My mind goes straight to our night in Oregon, our first time having sex. His hands gripping my arm. His weight on top of me.

His pupils dilate slightly as if he can read my mind. Then he blinks and returns to his conversation. That split-second glance leaves my breathing unsteady. I tear my eyes away as a shiver runs down my spine.

Maddie will find love. But—and it terrifies me to confess this—I may have already found it myself. Could I? Could I be in love with him? It's been such a whirlwind of adventure and disappointment and excitement and uncertainty. But it's not just what's happened to us—it's what's happened *within* us. The sweet, quiet moments we've shared. The way I feel I've come alive. There's so much more to come for us. Does he realize that too? It was all in that glance.

Two hands grip my shoulder from behind, and I jump.

"Ethan's an asshole."

Maddie goes to the empty seat on the other side of Devon and falls into it, draining her current glass of wine. She waves over a staff member holding a tray of brimming champagne flutes and takes one with haste. After a giant gulp, she leans forward across Devon to tell me, "He turned me down. Couldn't get a number or anything."

Devon leans back to give her room as my tipsy best friend invades his personal space to replay the events of her failed hookup. "He barely looked at me. And when he did, he was all, *'And you are?'* like I'm a nobody."

She settles back into her chair and drinks from her glass. The lights dim as a spotlight brings our focus to the stage. Rhyanne comes out and welcomes everyone to the Fifth Annual YOUTHelp Celebrity Gala. After a storm of applause, she recounts her own struggles being accepted as a transgender woman. Her childhood was filled with bullying from peers and discomfort from her own broken self-identity. When she got her big break, she knew she had to do more. And that's how YOUTHelp was born. Another round of applause erupts.

"Now let's get this gala started! We're fortunate to have Stone Records as a key sponsor, and here to perform "Only You", the one and only, Ethan Beckham."

Ethan takes Rhyanne's place on stage, wearing his trademark glasses—his guitar slung over his shoulder. A drummer and bassist sneak into the background and take their spots. I bite my lip and turn to face Maddie.

Her eyes glower as she finishes another glass of champagne and crosses her arms over her chest. Ethan starts to play, and she rolls her eyes and looks over to me.

Her lips form the word without a sound, Asshole.

CHAPTER TWELVE

I can't help but smile at Maddie's tantrum. She's gorgeous, and it's usually effortless for her to snag a guy's attention. Most men throw their numbers at her before she can bat a lash. Her exaggerated disappointment— enhanced by the alcohol, no doubt—is comical knowing she'll be over it by morning.

Ethan finishes his song, and Rhyanne comes back to remind us about the silent auction taking place in the back of the room. Then she asks that everyone take a moment to remember those who've not only experienced the harsh, violent acts of cruelty and discrimination, but those who didn't survive the hate.

My pulse quickens, the room falls into silence, and all I can hear is the thunderous shaking of my own inhale. I lower my head and squeeze my eyes shut. This is all for Jared and those like him.

Fingers interlock with my own, and I open my eyes to find Devon's soothing hand embracing mine. I look from him to Rhys. His eyes are filled with tears, but he gives me a reassuring smile.

Everything he and I went through years ago—separately, experiencing the trauma in isolation—yet here we are, going through this together. This is for Jared.

Rhyanne begins talking again, and I force a slow, deep breath through my lungs to relax the tension. The hard part is over. Now we reminisce and enjoy the evening.

Only it's not. Rhyanne goes straight into a speech delving into emotional anecdotes. A screen behind her illuminates the faces of young victims as she recollects their stories. I respect her, I do. She speaks with care and grace. It's clear this is her passion, and she's set on making a difference. But I know whose story she's going to tell.

Natalia got all the details from me a few days ago.

We're all going to live through Jared's untimely death. But these people didn't know him. They couldn't possibly understand the horror Rhys and I lived through.

It's hot in here. There are too many people and not enough oxygen. Face-after-face appear behind Rhyanne. A ten-year-old boy who attempted suicide. A fourteen-year-old girl who was tormented online for years until she ran away. I sip at my drink. As each photo switches to the next, I hold my breath anticipating the one face I'll know. My leg involuntarily bounces from the uncomfortable state of limbo.

A gentle nudge on my arm breaks me from the shackles of my anxious mind.

"Come with me," Devon whispers.

He grips my hand and casually leads us out of the room. Through the doors, he looks left, then right, and pulls me down an empty hallway until we're out of sight. Rhyanne's muffled voice travels through the walls but not well enough to hear what she's saying—or whose story she's telling.

"We need to get back in there. I don't want to be rude," I say.

"You don't have to put yourself through all that," he says. "You're here. You already know these problems exist, and you're here doing something about them. This part of it," he points back toward the ballroom, "that's not for you. That's for everyone else, to get them to understand. It's business for them. It's personal, and painful, for you. It's okay to skip this part."

Devon's right. I drop his hand and massage my temples. I can breathe out here. I take a moment to quiet my mind before speaking again. "Alright. I'm good now. Thank you."

"You're crying."

I bring my hand to my cheek to find it wet. Great. I'll be the one in there with the smeared makeup and red eyes while everyone else looks flawless.

Devon pulls my hands away from my face and kisses them. Then he brushes his fingers along my cheeks, removing the last of my tears. My breath catches as his thumb runs along my bottom lip.

That's it. Forget everything right now.

I close my eyes and lunge toward him, my mouth finding his. He kisses me slowly at first, but I'm hungry for more. I need an escape right now. I need Devon. He got me out of that room. But that only eased my mind. The rest of me needs more—yearns for more. I kiss him with force, and he backs me into the wall. Standing on my tiptoes, I turn my head. Devon moves to my neck, kissing, nibbling his way from my earlobe to my collarbone. My hands grope under his tux jacket, finding the firm contours of his abs. My manicured nails scratch their way around his waist and up his back.

With a shaky voice, I ask, "You said you have a penthouse upstairs?"

He moves back to my ear, his hot breath making me melt. My legs are weak, but every muscle throbs for him now.

I know he knows what I want. "Too far away," he answers and there's a mischievous spark in his eye.

Without hesitation, he takes my hand and pushes me toward the first door on the left. It's the stairwell leading up to the other floors. It's carpeted in plush red and lit with warm light from a pattern of brass sconces. I look up at the kaleidoscope effect of the illuminated stairs, dozens of levels growing smaller and smaller with each floor, and at the top, a square of stained glass window reveals the black of the night.

If a stairwell can be this alluring, what's waiting for us in the room where Devon's taking—

He presses me into the wall, leaning more of his weight into me than before in the hallway. His hands wrap around my hips and cup the flesh of my ass, pulling me against the hardness waiting in his pants. I grasp ahold of his jacket to keep myself standing. The door's closed behind us and all is quiet in here. But I don't want to waste time kissing. I want to reach our destination. I want him in me.

His mouth claims mine. I breathe him in, consumed.

The first chance I get to speak—as Devon's mouth skims over the exposed skin just above the bust of my gown—I confess, "I want you. Where can we go? I don't want to wait another second."

"Then don't."

His hands grab me harder and he lifts me up. My right heel finds the bottom step of the first floor staircase, and I use the leverage to push myself up higher. I tilt my hips, and yes, our bodies perfectly align.

But we can't do this here. "We'll get caught."

"We might." He teases my throbbing mound with his rock hard erection and nibbles at the soft skin of my breast. "You want to stop?"

I answer by pushing his jacket. That needs to come off. Now.

He lowers me long enough to remove it, tossing it onto the steps. The seconds my body is without him leave my burning skin mourning. I busy myself with the buttons of his shirt as Devon's hands explore. One finds the gown's slit right at my thigh. His fingers trail up to the tiny thong I'm wearing. He loops the strap around his index finger and pulls it away from my skin.

"Mmm," he groans approvingly and his hand continues to the front of me, where he firmly presses his fingers into the apex of my thighs.

Another moan, from both of us this time. He continues to play as his free hand strokes the back of my head, his fingers weaving into the careful up-do that won't stand a chance with Devon.

First the button of his pants. Then the zipper. This has to be quick, and right now, he's taking far too long to plunge inside of me. Before I can push his pants down, he reaches into a pocket and pulls out a condom.

How convenient. "Were you planning on this?" I tease.

"I'm always ready for you." He tears the wrapper, his eyes locked on me. "And I know you're ready for me."

My cheeks warm at the accusation. I listen again for any sign of company. I cannot be caught doing this. This is so not me.

Devon's hands are back on me, though, and I forget to even care. I'll take a whole audience if it means having him take me right this second.

He lifts me up again, and I dig my heel into the carpeted step while wrapping my other leg around Devon's waist. In a smooth, swift move, he frees himself from his boxers, moves my gown and thong out of the way, and buries himself in me to the hilt. A scream escapes me. Fuck. Someone had to have heard that.

I bite into Devon's shoulder to stifle any further sounds. He finds a steady rhythm, and I buck against him meeting his pace. The collection of diamonds that make up my elaborate necklace make a light, clinking sound— like the world's tiniest wind chime. I kiss him again. On his neck, his chin, his mouth. My lips linger over his as he watches my reaction to him filling me, massaging my most sensitive spots from the inside.

The first shudder courses through me, and I hear a door slam from somewhere upstairs.

My eyes go wide. "Someone's coming. We have to stop."

He smiles his sly half-grin. "Is that what you want?"

I look up, trying to see where the interruption came from. Three floors above us? Thirty floors?

Devon stops thrusting waiting for my response, but my body betrays me. He can't stop. I lift myself up and drop back down onto him, clenching my muscles to feel the fullness of his shaft. He buries his face into my neck and growls with ecstasy.

My senses are on fire. Everything is Devon. But we're seconds from being caught. Oh my god. What will the unsuspecting witness think finding two bodies screwing in the stairwell?

Footsteps.

They're getting closer. The hair raises on the back of my neck. I reach out grabbing for the stair rail, something to hold me up.

Devon thrusts harder, in and out. His chest heaves. His fingers dig into my flesh.

I'm going to fall. My whole body's gone weak.

More footsteps. Getting louder.

Devon pushes into me harder. Faster. Oh yes. He feels so good. But it's too much. The thrill of being somewhere so...public. The impending moment of being found. The humiliation. The urgency to keep quiet. The involuntary moans and sighs. The pleasure. The excitement.

I bite my lip and let all my focus move down to where Devon and I join as one.

The slick sounds of his movements are almost enough to push me overboard. He uses his teeth to slip my one strap off my shoulder. It falls, unveiling the top of the lacy, white corset.

The look of adoration on his face makes me forget about our intruder who definitely came from one of the higher floors. I listen again. The footsteps continue, and a shuffling sound tells me they're carrying something. A bag? A box?

Who cares? Devon nudges the diamonds aside and kisses my cleavage, running his tongue along my curving skin, leaving behind a trail of prickles.

I begin to shiver. The leg I have wrapped around Devon struggles to hold on. The leg supporting me on the step shakes and threatens to give in before the rest of my body comes undone.

But Devon has me. His strong hands hold me in place, unrelenting. He's moving faster now, and the shakiness of his own breathing tells me he's just as close as I am.

"Come for me, Olivia." His voice is rough, low. Demanding.

My head drops down onto his. The fire builds inside me, inching through my veins. Another shudder, a tremor, and I moan, this time louder.

The footsteps stop for a second. I freeze, paralyzed against the wall. If I stay still, maybe they'll go away.

But Devon doesn't stop. No, instead he pulls himself out as far as our limited space allows, and then dives deep into me. The second time he does it, I feel myself convulse around him.

An "oh" escapes me, and now I know we're busted. I hold my breath, waiting for whatever happens next. I try to contain my impending orgasm, the tension growing stronger and more certain by the second. A throat clears from the floor above us. A door opens. A door closes. Silence.

We're alone again.

Devon slowly thrusts a third, agonizing time, and I cry out as a soul-shattering orgasm finally pushes me over the edge. As I come, he thrusts harder and harder until his own release pulses into me.

His writhing slows, and every movement sends another shockwave through my body until we both settle and he releases me.

I lean my head into the wall, catching my breath. My dress is all out of place. My half-naked breasts shine with a sheen of sweat. My hair is falling down.

"You're beautiful," Devon says.

I laugh, all tension and emotion from the gala long gone. "I look like I was just ravaged by Devon Stone. I'm a mess."

"You're beautiful," he repeats.

Devon gets himself dressed and helps me put myself back together. He even twists my disheveled curls and gets them pinned back into place. My hero.

CHAPTER THIRTEEN

"Ready"? Devon asks.

We managed to have sex in a stairwell without being *completely* caught, but now comes the final challenge. We might open this door to find a crowd's gathered. What then?

Devon kisses me one last time and checks outside. "Coast is clear."

I sigh with relief, and then giggling takes over. *That* just happened. So much for only talking. Stepping out into the hall, we head toward the restrooms to freshen up before re-turning to the gala. One look in the mirror, and it's more than obvious that I just had sex. My eyes are heavy, lips swollen red, mascara smeared down my cheek.

I laugh again and get to work making my-self look more presentable. I erase all the evi-dence and use a wet towel to cool my neck and shoulders.

All better.

Before I can pull the door open to leave, it's shoved toward me and I jump back to avoid being slammed into.

Maddie rushes past, not noticing me, and locks herself in the largest stall. Seconds lat-er, I hear her vomit.

There goes my mood.

"Madd, you alright?"

"Olivia?"

"Yeah, you almost knocked me out with that door." I wait by the sinks as she finishes and comes out looking like hell.

"I think I drank too much."

She thinks? The poor girl's eyes are blood-shot, her face paler than a corpse, and she's trembling all over. I grab another towel, soaking it with the coldest water I can get from the faucet. She comes over and rests her elbows on the countertop, her head in her hands.

"I feel like shit."

"I know, honey." I run the towel over her neck. "Please tell me this isn't all because of Ethan Beckham."

"Who?" She shakes her head after a second. "No, not that ass. Not even Corey. Things just...suck right now. I see how you're doing. How your life is...accelerating. Mine seems to be stuck at a red light."

Sort of poetic for a drunk girl. I need to help her, but I have no words of wisdom right now. She's always been the one helping me, not the other way around.

She reaches one shaky hand out to hold mine. "Can we go home? I just need my bed."

"Of course." Can I leave this early? I could probably sneak out with no one noticing. Though at the very least, I need to find Natalia and probably Rhyanne and say goodbye.

I help Maddie out of the bathroom and we find Devon waiting outside the gala doors.

"What happened to her?"

Maddie hangs onto my arm as if I'm her lifeline. "She went a little overboard, that's all. I have to get her home."

Rhys and Christopher come out the doors and almost run into us.

"There you are," Rhys says. "I'm sorry to cry and run, but we need to head out. It's a long drive back, and—"

"Yeah. No worries," I say.

So Maddie needs to leave. Rhys needs to leave. They're going in opposite directions, so I guess this ends our night. It was certainly a memorable one, to say the least. It was too fast though.

Devon comes around and takes Maddie's other arm. "How about you stay? I'll give her a ride back."

He doesn't have to do that. "You sure? I don't know how much longer this thing is. It's really not a big deal."

"No, it's your night. Stick around. Enjoy the spotlight."

I smile and look back to Rhys and Christopher. "I wish we had more time to visit."

"We'll be back. Next time, we'll get together and hang out without all the extravagant stuff. Deal?"

I give Rhys the tightest hug I can muster. "Deal." My eyes are brimming with tears. "It's been so good seeing you again."

"You too."

We finish our goodbyes, and I watch them head out. Life can throw such awful curve balls. But look how wonderful things can turn out.

Okay, all but Maddie. She probably wouldn't categorize anything as wonderful right this moment. She groans, and I feel nothing but sympathy. "Okay, get her home. Fast, before she hurls in your car."

"She even thinks about it, and I'm kicking her ass to the curb."

He might mean that, so I give him a quick kiss and tell him to go.

"Hey. I can grab some clothes from your room while I'm there. We can stay in the penthouse overnight." He nods toward the ceiling.

I consider the idea of him rummaging through my underwear drawer. Oh well, I don't have anything to hide from him. "I thought we agreed to just talk later?"

"Yeah. We'll talk. We can continue the conversation we started in the stairwell."

My skin flushes. There was no conversation in there. Only...

He reaches into his back pocket, pulling out his wallet. Digging through, he finds a hotel key and hands it to me. "Top floor. You can't miss it. So you enjoy yourself," he says.

"I'll make sure she gets home, and I'll see you later." His eyes stay on me a moment longer, and a schoolgirl grin forces itself across my face.

There's no denying. I've fallen for this guy.

I reenter the gala feeling like I'm floating on a cloud. The guests don't notice I've been gone—a perk to not *actually* being a celebrity—and I'm just in time to hear the winners of the silent auction. I take my seat at our now empty table and watch all the action. Rhyanne lists all the prizes, the recipients cheer, and a digital meter on the screen behind her updates with the amount of money raised for the foundation. Seriously, someone bid a half million dollars on a year-long spa membership. I've said bad things before about celebrities and their frivolous lifestyle, but if tonight's taught me anything (besides how much fun impulsive, stairwell sex is) it's that these Hollywood types do have a generous heart to match their overflowing wallet. I pull my phone from my bag to see if Devon's called. No notifications, but I'm worried about Maddie, so I keep it grasped in my hand, just in case.

The gala comes to a successful end soon after. The partygoers pile out and the clean up crew takes over. I finally spot Natalia checking something on a tablet.

I grab my clutch, adjusting its strap around my wrist and walk over to her, "Hey."

She looks up, surprised. "You're still here. That's great."

"Yeah, I wanted to thank you. This week's been a new experience for me. You made it really great."

"Oh no problem. It's my job, after all." She moves to a table stacked with boxes and lifts one.

"Can I at least help you pick up or—"

"Oh no, you were a guest, not a staff member." The box is heavier than she expected, and she waivers on her heels. "Though, if you find a strange enjoyment out of loading a truck, you're more than welcome to suit yourself."

I laugh at the underlying plea for help. In a not-very-ladylike gesture, I turn and shove my phone down into my cleavage to free my hands, push the strap of my clutch up to my elbow to keep it out of the way, and grab one side of the box, assisting Natalia out a back entrance. A white moving truck waits, its back door open.

"Where'd Devon disappear to? We could use some of that muscle power."

"He's helping a friend. He's got a penthouse here, so if you want to wait, he'll be back, and I'm sure he'd be willing to help out if you need anything. It's the least we could do."

"I think you and I can make do."

A few trips later, we've loaded boxes filled with linens, decorations, and centerpieces. The rest of the staff loads tables and chairs into a separate truck, and I'm reminded how quick and efficient event planners can be.

"See? Girl power," Natalia says, smiling. "And in heels, no less."

We're loading the projector screen into the back of the truck, me pulling it to the back, Natalia pushing. She climbs up and moves a few boxes around to make sure things won't fall over while driving.

I sit on one of the closed boxes to catch my breath. Devon still hasn't called, but he must be on his way back by now. "So let me know if you ever need me for anything like this again. In fact," I lean down and fix the strap of one of my heels and stand back up, "if the non-profit needs anyone, you know, full time or something, I'd love to get involved."

I'm expecting a response from Natalia as she multitasks.

When she doesn't answer, I turn back toward her to see if she needs help with anything. A sudden, searing pain shoots through my skull, and stars flash across the dark metal of the truck. I fall back, not knowing what happened. I grab my head with my hands and pull away, blood staining my fingers.

I open my mouth to speak, to call for help, but my vision blurs, and I can't get any words out. As the scene above me sways in and out of focus, I piece it together. Natalia stands over me, one of the wooden placards in her hand.

What the—?

She raises her hands over her head to strike me again.

I throw a hand up. "No!" A streetlight reflects off the image printed on the solid wood. My own brother looks back at me, frozen in the past.

What did I miss? How is this happening? Natalia's been nothing but nice. *Why* is she doing this? What did I do?

"Nothing against you, darling. You have no idea how long it's taken to get this close to Devon again. You're the only thing in my way."

Devon? None of this makes sense. My head throbs. I close my eyes.

Devon. Devon's with Maddie.

Maddie. Maddie arguing with Natalia.

Natalia. At the apartment, coming out of my room. She said she couldn't find the bathroom.

"She can track down your apartment, but she can't find a room with a toilet?" Maddie had said that.

What had Natalia been doing in my room?

"I know it's you ... The phone calls." Devon said I'd been calling him.

That long list of unknown numbers and no voice at the other end.

Natalia. She's been after Devon this whole time?

But...then who the hell is she? And what does she want now?

I pry my eyes open, determined to confront her. To stop her. Somehow.

The look in her eyes is nothing but pure hatred as Natalia's hands come down with a force I'm too weak to fight against. Another slam into my head. The corner of the solid wood hits my temple.

Everything goes black.

THE LUST LIST: DEVON STONE

FOUR LETTERS

MIRA BAILEE

Available Now

THE LUST LIST

The Lust List - Take Your Pick
They're the world's sexiest bachelors. The men of *ScandalLust* mag's infamous Lust List are young, wealthy, and, oh, did we mention? *Hot*.

When scandal follows them everywhere, there's no hiding from the cameras. They're irresistible, insatiable—and talented in all the right ways. Every woman wants them. But these playboys won't be easy to catch...

THE LUST LIST DEVON STONE

by MIRA BAILEE

FIRST TASTE
SECOND CHANCES
THIRD DEGREE
FOUR LETTERS

Acknowledgments

Without a doubt, I have the best support team by my side. I'm eternally grateful for the following spectacular individuals:

My writing partner, Nova Raines. I wouldn't be doing this without you.

My editor, Nicole Bailey (Proof Before You Publish); my cover designer, Qamber Designs; and my beta readers. You all are the reason my books are any good.

My family and friends whose support doesn't waiver, no matter the genre I write.

And all my readers. Your enthusiasm helps me breathe life into every new book.

Thank you.

About Mira Bailee

Mira Bailee, a beer-brewing librarian, has been writing leisurely, scholarly, and professionally for the past twenty years.

While she's always maintained a high standard of chaos in her daily routine, *The Lust List* allows her to pass on some of her hectic lifestyle to her characters. Her storytelling balances humor and pleasure with sincerity and conflict, providing a wild ride of human emotions.

In the past she studied filmmaking and screenwriting and determined what goes on behind the scenes is just as tantalizing as what's seen in front of the camera. This revelation is the basis for her inspiration for *The Lust List.*